RAPTURE:
SINS OF THE SINNER

A.C. Henley and Fran Heckrotte

Affinity
eBook Press
NZ

Acknowledgments

When Rapture, Sins of the Sinners was born, AC Henley's health was failing. We both knew it was a good plotline and it was easy for her to get her vision on paper. She would talk with me about it over my morning coffee, always asking if I understood where she wanted the story to go. The hard part was when she would ask me to finish it for her should she pass away, leaving the work unfinished. I always reassured her that I would finish it on the outside chance that she would leave it undone. When AC left for another unworldly plane, Rapture (as we fondly refer to the story) sat for more than a year untouched – not even thought of, the furthest thing from my mind.

AC's yahoo group's fan base (henleyac) knew it was a good story and they enjoyed reading all the tidbits they were thrown and encouraged me to finish Rapture. It's true I am a writer, but I write romances, I knew there was no way that I could finish it. Enter Fran Heckrotte. Fran and AC had many late night conversations, both writers too busy to sleep. I knew Fran saw AC's vision and I asked her if she was interested in finishing the manuscript, for I knew she was the one person that saw Rapture the way AC and I did. When Fran agreed, we immediately began to look at the skeleton that AC left behind and she rolled up her sleeves, so to speak, made me roll mine up, too, and we began to put flesh on the bones that is Rapture.

It was a good marriage, Fran and Rapture. She knew the manuscript from her chats with AC and she took the story and ran with it, pulling me – often dragging me - along with her. Oh, Fran would give me assignments or ask me to read something, yet I take no credit other than bringing the two together. This book would not have happened had it not been for Fran Heckrotte's dedication to her friend, and I'm sure wherever AC is right this moment, she's smiling at you, Fran. I would like to say that AC brought Fran and I together, and I consider her one of my dear friends. I would like to meet you one day and shake your hand.

Thank you for all your dedication and hard work, Fran...s.

A Note From Co-author Fran Heckrotte

AC Henley had a dream; one that would never have been fulfilled if Sherry, her partner, hadn't stepped in to make it come true. Rapture, Sins of the Sinner, is the culmination of Sherry's determination and collaboration over a long period of time. This is a story that could not be rushed. Sherry understood the importance of getting it right first before having it published. Thanks, kiddo, for your patience, your insight and your dedication to making Bri's dream a reality.

And to all the others who encouraged us or have been involved as beta readers, copy editors, cover artists, and the rest of the Affinity family, thank you.

Fran Heckrotte

Dedication

Bridgette Wyman

aka AC Henley

1967 - 2009

Table of Contents

Chapter 1

Houston, Texas

Big cities offered anonymity. They are the kind of places that provided the faceless, nameless interactions she craved, and then later hated herself for indulging in.

Looking at the list of nearby churches she had hastily jotted down from the phonebook, Agnes Kelly-Elliott left her hotel room, making sure the door was secured. It was dark out, but the streetlamps provided sufficient light to feel reasonably safe. Come morning, she would have need of a priest before catching the plane back to Ft. Worth, not that confessing her sins would do her any good. They were a part of her, something that could never be purged by penitent prayers. Pleasure and release were addictive. Neither could be ignored for long.

Agnes dreaded these trips, yet could not deny her cravings. Life would be unbearable if her family or co-workers found out about her secret weekends away from her hometown. The church would be the only thing left to offer her solace. She tried hard to control a vice that was impossible to ignore.

†

The half-lit neon sign above over the doors entrance flickered.

Sophie's Choice, she thought. "They really need to fix that light," Agnes mumbled, remembering she had said the same thing the night before when she checked out the place. This bar was perfect for what she required. A lesbian bar, the odds were good she'd find just the right partner for a few hours of pleasure. *Six weeks*. Certainly not a record for abstinence, but it was a long stretch. Her job provided few opportunities to pursue personal wants or needs.

Shoving the list she had been clutching tightly in her hand into her back pocket, Agnes pushed open the door to the bar. Although she had been taking these types of trips for a few years, she could never get over the initial jitters.

The dark interior provided a comfortable level of anonymity, calming her nerves. The smell of perfume and cologne was the first thing she noticed but it couldn't conceal the dirty smell of tobacco. A misty smoke swirled lazily around the room. Feeling queasy, she unconsciously rubbed her stomach. Her blood raced, first in anticipation of what lay ahead, and then with guilt. Guilt! It gnawed at her gut like a bad enchilada. Slowly she made her way deeper into the darkness, ignoring anyone that looked like a regular. Agnes was on a mission and they had no place in her plans.

"A Cosmo," she called out to the bartender. Pulling a twenty-dollar bill from her shirt pocket, Agnes laid it on the bar before turning to check out the dimly lit room. The place was like many others she had visited, small and intimate. Several customers gave her the once-over before returning to their conversations.

Guess I don't fit their needs either. Most of the seats around the tables were taken. A few loners were scattered about. *Probably looking for the same thing I am.* These were the women that interested Agnes—potential candidates for the evening. Someone was always available for a one-night stand. All Agnes had to do was find the right person.

The jukebox played k.d. lang's "Shadowland." Couples swayed intimately on the cozy wooden dance floor. Unconsciously, Agnes moved slightly to the tune.

"Would you like to dance?"

Startled, Agnes jumped. She hadn't even realized someone was standing so close. Forcing a smile, she turned.

Nice! She was relieved to see an attractive woman dressed in simple black trousers and a white western style shirt. Pale blue eyes sparkled.

"I just ordered." Agnes pointed to the money lying on the counter.

"It'll be here when we get back," the woman said as she leaned against the bar. Her long dark hair was pushed behind her ears and hung down past her shoulders, giving Agnes an unobstructed view of her face.

Agnes usually avoided women who tried to pick her up. It usually meant they wanted to be in control. There was something about this one, though, that was different, or at least felt that way.

"All right. One dance." When the woman held out her hand, Agnes reluctantly clasped it. Her eyes traveled along the tanned, outstretched arm and upward.

Gotta be at least six feet. At five eight Agnes didn't consider herself to be short. Having to look up, though, was a bit disconcerting.

"Can I ask your name?"

"You can but…" Agnes said as she found herself pulled close to the lean body. Their height difference did have some advantages. Her head rested easily on the cotton-covered shoulder.

"But what?"

"Before I tell you, there're a few requirements." Agnes knew she was moving fast. Perhaps it was her need driving her, but if she could take control quickly, she might have found what she was looking for.

"Hmm. So do I fulfill these…requirements?"

The question was whispered directly into Agnes's ear. She shivered as the warm breath caressed her cheek, and pressed closer into the embrace. Shifting slightly, she began to lead their slow dance. Agnes glanced at the woman's face to judge her reaction.

"You do, so far. If you want to accompany me…" Without thinking Agnes placed a soft, lingering kiss on her dance partner's slightly parted lips, then eased out of the embrace and moved toward the bar. Collecting her change she sipped the cocktail that was next to it. Moments later, her dance partner returned.

"I'm not looking for more than tonight," Agnes warned, "and no contact afterward. No exchanging phone numbers, no addresses, no nothing. We've never met."

"Perfect!" the woman said. "I like simple."

Agnes smiled and downed the rest of her drink. She tipped the bartender.

"My hotel's not far. Care to walk me there?"

"In this neighborhood?"

"I'll protect you." Agnes reached out, wrapping her hand around a rock hard bicep. "Although you seem well equipped to take care of yourself."

"I do all right." The woman smiled exposing straight white teeth.

"I bet you do."

Agnes held her hand out. The woman took it without hesitation. Things were working out well.

The humid Houston air settled on her as soon as she stepped outside. She immediately dropped the woman's hand. Agnes wished she had a bit more nerve in public. Home was a few hundred miles away. The chances of anyone knowing her here were slim to none but she wasn't chancing an accidental discovery.

Neither spoke as they walked the five blocks to the hotel. The neighborhood transitioned from tacky to more prominent housing. It was often a dichotomy to Agnes that the haves and the have-nots could live in such close proximity, and yet be oblivious to each other's lifestyles.

"What are you in town for?"

Agnes hated questions, but couldn't always ignore them even though it was necessary to maintain her anonymity. Of course, there was nothing to stop her from telling a few small lies. She made a mental note to add that sin to her confessions in the morning.

"Business."

"You clearly don't like questions. Is that one of the requirements?"

"Not exactly but it's better this way. We're here." Agnes smiled her thanks to the night porter when he opened the door for them.

The foyer was polished marble; the elevator, polished stainless steel giving her an excellent view of them standing together. Agnes's hair was more red than blonde. She had often suffered through nicknames like 'ginger' and 'carrot top' growing up. Her hair color was a sharp contrast to the woman standing beside her who happened to be looking directly at her in the reflection. Smiling sheepishly Agnes blushed and looked away.

Busted!

The hotel room was roomy and comfortable. Normally a simple motel served her purpose but this trip she had splurged, a long overdue treat. Selfishness would have to be added to the growing list of sins. She motioned toward the king-sized bed.

"Make yourself comfortable. Would you like something to drink?" The woman looked at the bed then back at Agnes.

"Are we going to go through pleasantries after all those requirements?"

"No need. Business it is." Agnes smiled thinly and kicked off her shoes. Tugging her blouse from her jeans she began unbuttoning it from the bottom.

"I like business. Pleasantries can be fun but tend to be tedious." The woman unbuttoned her own shirt, pulling the tails from her black trousers. She unhooked her large gold belt buckle, unsnapped and unzipped her pants. Sitting down on the bed she bent over and grabbed a boot.

Agnes felt her blood racing.

"What's your name?"

"So you get to ask questions, now?" Before Agnes could reply the woman relented. "Cochise." A powerful tug sent the boot thudding to the floor.

"Like the Apache?"

The other boot hit the floor. "Who else?"

"Interesting." Agnes pushed the top of her jeans down her hips.

"And yours?"

"Kelly."

Cochise stood and pulled her shirt off, draping it neatly over the headboard, barely noticing a rosary draped over its corner.

"Irish?"

"You might say that." Agnes left her panties and bra on as she crossed the room to stand in front of Cochise. "Apache?" Agnes asked. Cochise clearly had some classic American Native features.

"You might say that."

Agnes chuckled. Her finger traveled from the top of Cochise's white sports bra to the waist of her pants.

"Take everything off and lay in the middle of the bed," Agnes ordered. "Please," she added as an afterthought. The pleasantry was merely a formality.

"You're very bossy."

"My game, my rules." Agnes waited for Cochise to comply before joining her. Sitting astride Cochise's abdomen, she settled her weight on the hips. Agnes felt the anticipated thrill of the conquest as she looked down at the woman under her. "Put your hands above your head."

"Why?" Cochise demanded, her voice tinged with suspicion.

Agnes took each of Cochise's wrists and gently forced them above the prone woman's head.

"Because I wish it." Agnes smiled. "And since I'm on top, I'm in control. Is that a problem?" She watched the play of emotions cross Cochise's face. "I'll allow you a safe word."

"You'll *allow*?"

"Yes, allow. I *am* in control, remember? That's one of the rules." She lowered her chest to Cochise's moving slowly forward and then back, eliciting a soft moan from the woman under her.

"Apache," Cochise rasped raggedly.

Agnes laughed. "How appropriate."

Agnes settled fully on top of Cochise and reached above her head for the two straps she had placed there earlier in the day. The Velcro closures that were wrapped around the frame were strong. They had never failed. Securing each strap to Cochise's wrists, she saw the hands ball into fists.

"I won't hurt you," she whispered. "This is a game, remember? It's all about pleasure."

"I...I don't even know you."

"You know my name. You know you want sex as much as I do, and you thought I was good enough for a one-night stand. What else do you need?" Kelly asked, planting kisses along Cochise's neck.

"I…" Cochise pulled hard at the restraints causing the headboard to creak. The edges of the leather cuffs pressed into her skin. "This is a mistake! I can't do this! Take these things off! Now!" Struggling against the restraints, Cochise flipped Agnes to the side. "Apache!" she cried out.

Stunned, Agnes scrambled to unfasten the buckles on the cuffs. It took longer than normal because of the woman's agitation. When the second cuff finally relented, she hurriedly moved away.

"I'm sorry! I thought you understood."

"Understood?" Cochise rose and hurried to the neat pile of clothes she had discarded a few minutes earlier. "You didn't say anything about *this*. At least have the guts to bring up your perversions before you invite someone to your room."

"Perversions? You're over—"

"You need a label, lady, something to warn people off since you apparently don't. Not everyone is into this type of thing." Cochise began to dress, finally sitting on the edge of the bed to pull her boots on. "What exactly is your problem anyway? The good old-fashioned way too boring for you?"

"I don't have a problem," Agnes said, barely able to control her own temper. "I told you earlier. I like control."

Cochise pulled on her second boot, stomping it against the floor.

"Control! This goes beyond control. You know what I think? I think you're nuts. If this is what you need to have sex, you're pathetic. Hell, you probably objectify women to deal with your sexuality. Still closeted, I bet. You're afraid someone else might be better than you. Control you. That's why you like tying women up!"

"You don't know anything about me," Agnes said, her voice turning cold. "Are you a shrink or something?"

"No, but it sure doesn't take a psychiatrist to figure this out." Cochise stood, zipped up her pants and buckled the belt. "You'd better hope you never run into someone else like you. It'll be quite an awakening."

Agnes wanted to object, but the woman was uncomfortably close to the truth. Dropping her gaze to the floor, she didn't know how to respond. The thought of giving control to another person was terrifying.

"Look, I'm sorry. I honestly thought you…"

Cochise had already made it to the door but stopped and turned.

"Thought what? That I'm into your weird stuff? I don't mind giving up control occasionally but I'll be damned if I'd let a complete stranger tie me up. What's your real name, anyway? At least have the decency to tell me that."

Agnes didn't look at her. "You know everything you need to know," she said.

Cochise gave a bitter laugh.

"Have it your way, Kelly." Yanking open the door she left, shutting it firmly behind her.

Agnes sat on the edge of the bed in silence. The evening was a disaster. She sighed. *Not exactly what I was hoping for,* she thought. Standing she pulled on her pants and blouse. After dressing, she straightened the bedding, and gave the room one last check. Glancing at her watch, she shrugged.

No use thinking about what didn't happen. Woman's a fruitcake. Oh well, the night's still young. Plenty of time to find someone more amenable.

And so she did. A young woman at the same bar where she had picked up Cochise, only this one was more cooperative and very eager.

Chapter 2

Five months later

Ft. Worth would always play second fiddle to Dallas when it came to Texas cities. It wasn't as big, it wasn't as flashy, it certainly wasn't as rich, and it didn't have a professional football team. Most of the residents didn't give a rat's ass. Ft. Worth was home.

That was how Agnes Kelly-Elliott felt. She went to college, married, raised her children, got divorced, and worked there. She'd probably die in Ft. Worth. Twenty years of service to the police department sealed her loyalty to the place she had always called home.

Her ex-husband was also a police officer—a beat cop. Griffin Elliott was a fourth generation Ft. Worth policeman. His family was well known in the department. Devoted and dependable cops, they were respected by almost everyone.

The first eight years of their marriage seemed perfect, and then Griff had an affair. Why, Agnes never understood, but felt she had somehow failed him and the marriage. At least in the beginning. The fact that his decision came on the heels of Agnes's promotion to detective didn't go unnoticed by her friends. When he declared his love for the other woman, the ensuing divorce was quick, quiet, and mutually agreed on.

Six months later Agnes had her first relationship with a woman. Whether it was from loneliness or something else didn't matter at the time. What did was a need to feel again.

†

Patty had been easy to talk to, sympathetic and emotionally supportive. Agnes felt… comfortable. The affair, if it could be called that, lasted several months. Mostly it was quiet dinners together followed by intimate moments. She learned more about her body in those six months than the eight years with Griff.

Eventually both realized nothing would come from their relationship. The sex had been good but neither felt the passion. They just weren't right for each other. Patty wished her the best and moved on.

More confused than ever, Agnes continued to question who and what she was. Men no longer held her interest but she wasn't willing to accept that she might be a lesbian. If her family ever found out about her affair, they would disown her. Still, what she had felt in Patty's arms made her yearn for something more. The pleasure was like an addiction, and like all addictions, needed to be satisfied.

Her only recourse was to feed her habit as far away from Ft. Worth as possible. Having a secret life was inconvenient but necessary.

✝

Agnes stood straight, shoulders back, chin up. She looked eloquent in her dress uniform, the medals on her chest a proud symbol of her success in a predominantly man's world.

Goddamn, I wish this was over with, she thought and then instantly regretted using His name in vain.

The chief of police rambled on and on about duty and civic pride. A few people in the audience yawned. Agnes clenched her jaw trying to stop herself from repeating the action. Hoping to distract herself from the boredom, she scanned the audience searching for familiar faces and mentally smiled when she saw her son and daughter sitting in the front row beside her parents. She winked at her daughter who acknowledged the gesture with a little finger wave.

Agnes took a deep breath wishing the chief wasn't so long-winded. A movement at the back of the room caught her attention.

Griff! He was leaning casually against the rear wall. As usual his dark blue uniform was slightly crumpled. When he was a beat cop his uniform had always looked crisp. Now that he was in Traffic and Patrol, he often had a slightly disheveled look, not that it ever bothered him. Griff always had the "don't fuck with me" air.

Agnes gave him a slight nod. Griff gave her a thumbs-up. It would be the only form of congratulations she would receive from him or his family. Officers above the rank of sergeant weren't to be trusted. The promotion to lieutenant was pretty much the final nail in the coffin as far as the Elliott clan was concerned. She was already persona non grata because of the divorce. Why they blamed her, she didn't understand, but that was all water under the bridge.

✝

When the moment came to receive her lieutenant bars, Agnes stepped forward. The chief pinned them on her collar, shook her hand, and moved to the next officer.

Finally, she thought. She hated ceremonies. It was a waste of time. The hours spent preparing for the promotion, listening to the speech, and for what? Ten seconds of formality.

Dinner with her parents and children was pleasant but uneventful. Her kids were both at university, choosing to stay on their respective campuses rather than at home. After her divorce, she and Griff agreed to a flexible joint custody. When one worked the nightshift, the other kept Matthew and Robin. They split the holidays and weekends. Vacations were often up for grabs. Most of the time, Agnes kept them, although occasionally Griff took them when she wanted a few days off to herself.

With the children gone, the three-bedroom house felt empty, the nights lonely. Getting away from the silence was more important than ever. Even an overnight in Dallas was a welcome relief. Twenty-eight miles was closer than she liked, but the club was decent and certainly better than nothing.

✝

Agnes removed her uniform, carefully draping it around a hanger.
I need some tea.

Heading toward the kitchen, she grabbed the *Star-Telegram.* Both would keep her company until she fell asleep. She had just settled into her bed when the phone rang.

What now? The green glowing numbers on the clock said it was just after eleven. Good news never came this late.

✝

The Stockyards of Ft. Worth was north of the city's center in a historic district popular with locals and visitors alike. Rodeos and special events offered the public a taste of the old west.

10

The crime scene wasn't hard to find. Blue and red flashing lights lit up the night creating an easy beacon to follow. Several police cars and an ambulance were already on-site. Agnes pulled her beige, unmarked car behind a parked police cruiser and sighed. Sleep deprived, the last eighteen hours were taking their toll on her. She wished she could just crawl back into bed.

Cool January air filled her lungs, helping to clear her head as she wove her way through the officers and technicians who were already collecting evidence. Then she saw it—the white sheet spread over the victim. In her ten years working homicide she was still uncomfortable seeing a lifeless body, especially people who died of unnatural causes. Agnes reached into her coat pocket for her notepad and pen. Crouching next to the body, she flipped through several pages searching for an empty page.

"Hey Elliott! Or should I call you lieutenant now?" a voice called out.

Agnes looked up and nodded at the man coming toward her from across a set of railroad tracks.

"Hey, Jeff." Agnes decided to ignore the question. He was her partner. Formality was the last thing they needed to worry about. "What do you know?" Agnes lifted the edge of the sheet, tipping her head sideways to peek at the body hidden underneath.

Jeff Roberts was young, fresh, and enthusiastic about his job. He'd made detective six months earlier. Homicides were still exciting; catching the bad guys a challenge unencumbered by the inevitable guilt of frequent failure. Like everyone who saw senseless death over and over, he too would eventually grow jaded about life and the world.

Opening his own notebook Jeff read off the facts he had scribbled down.

"White female, probably mid-twenties, blonde, blue eyes, and built."

Agnes let the sheet drop and pulled a pair of latex gloves from her jeans pocket.

"Built? Is that how you're going to describe her in your report?"

"Sorry. I mean fit. She appears very fit."

"Any witnesses?" Agnes decided to let the issue drop. Grabbing the sheet, she threw it off to the side.

"None yet. A mounted officer found her around ten thirty. He was checking the tracks."

"A body and no witnesses. Not a good start."

"And no clear evidence so far. We found three crack pipes, two old condoms, and forty-eight cigarette butts in the immediate area. Donny took the pictures already and the techs have bagged everything for forensics. I doubt if those will do us much good, though," Jeff added with a cynical smile.

So the real world has set in, Agnes thought. *The sooner the better.*

"You never know," she replied in a futile effort to make him feel a little better. "Killers aren't perfect no matter how good they are at cleaning up their messes. I'll need a minute here." Jeff nodded and walked away. Agnes opened her notebook, drew a diagram, and started taking notes. The dead woman was naked and laying on her back. Her head was pointing west. The arms were tied across her chest, with her hands pressed together as if she were praying. Red marks around her wrists and ankles indicated that the woman had been bound. Agnes recognized the pattern. A bruise on one thigh looked like a handprint. Positioning her hand over it without touching the skin, she saw it was smaller than hers. She described in detail her observations, sketching each location of anything unusual. Leaning closer to examine the face she frowned. *Why are your eyes like that?* Dead people often seemed to stare into the unknown but this woman's seemed unnaturally wide open. Not daring to touch the body, she made a note to ask the medical examiner about this then pulled out her small pocket camera to snap a few pictures.

"My pictures are never good enough for you, are they Elliott?"

Agnes shrugged, recognizing the voice.

"Hi, Donny. You know how I am. I don't like having to wait for photos."

The photographer grimaced.

"Not my fault I'm overworked. Congrats on the bars by the way. You deserve them." His camera clicked as he started taking pictures.

"Do me a favor." Agnes pointed to a group of people congregated nearby. "Take a few of those rubberneckers. It's a bit late for them to be hanging around here. And get a couple of the uniforms to make field cards on them. We might be able to match some DNA with the evidence picked up, or at least see if any of them have a history."

"Sure thing." Donny changed lenses and adjusted the focus, clicking off a half-dozen shots. "I'll have the pics for you tomorrow afternoon."

"I won't hold my breath," Agnes said mostly to herself. "Thanks, Donny." She headed over to join Jeff who was talking to the mounted police officer. Jeff smiled at her as she came to a stop next to him.

"Lt. Kelly-Elliott, this is Cpl. Macks. He found the body."

Agnes reached out and shook the man's gloved hand. She looked up at the officer's horse standing patiently by its rider.

"Beautiful animal," she started conversationally. Even veteran police officers could become spooked by the sight of a lifeless body. "How long have you been with the mounted force?"

"Eight months, ma'am," he said with pride. "I transferred from Traffic and Patrol."

"I worked mounted for a year shortly after joining the department." Agnes remembered the time fondly and smiled. "Is this your regular beat?"

"Yes ma'am. I check the tracks every night between ten and eleven. There was a big to-do at the White Elephant Saloon down the road. Sometimes they wander over here for other activities."

Activities involving crack pipes and condoms, Agnes thought. "Would you write it all down tonight while it's fresh? I know you're already an hour over your shift but it's important I get your report quickly. We won't keep you any longer than we have to."

The officer tipped his hat to her politely.

"Certainly ma'am. I mean lieutenant. I'll have a report for you after I get Maggie settled in her stall."

"Thanks." Agnes shook the man's hand again and watched as he mounted his horse. After he rode off, she turned to Jeff. "I don't like this. The body and the scene are too clean. Too neat. She wasn't killed here."

"My thoughts exactly." Jeff yawned.

"Are you done?" Her partner looked tired. Normally he was full of energy. She certainly didn't want him off sick. They were already overloaded with other investigations. "I can handle the rest of this. Go home."

Jeff glanced at his notes before shrugging.

"I think I'll check out the crowd first. Then I'm out of here. See you later."

Agnes looked at her watch.

"Okay. I'm going to look around some more. This is a risky place to dump a body if Cpl. Macks is right. Too many people hanging about. The killer had to know that, which means he wanted the body found." *This victim had been staged.* She had read about similar murders on the statewide law-enforcement alert site.

Chapter 3

Nearly three hundred miles south in San Antonio, Cochetta Lovejoy pulled her Bronco into her assigned parking space at Ranger Company D's field office. It was five a.m. and she felt cheated of sleep. On a normal day she was extremely intolerant of idiots. Pity the fool that crossed her path today. Grabbing her tanned leather briefcase, she slid off the seat to the pavement below. She stamped her feet to settle her jeans over her boots then turned back to retrieve her white Stetson. Cochetta promptly placed it on her head, automatically tipping it slightly forward to shade her eyes.

The office was nearly deserted as she made her way to her desk. There was a pile of messages on her keyboard. Shuffling through them, she absentmindedly reached over to turn on her PC.

What a bunch of crap! She thought tossing the messages to the side.

Within minutes she was scanning her e-mails, ignoring those that didn't have priority subject lines. As usual, that meant most of them.

"You're in early," her supervisor said, resting his butt against the edge of her desk.

Cochetta didn't even look up. One e-mail in particular had caught her attention.

"Hey, Captain," she said finally acknowledging his presence. "Looks like they found another one in Ft. Worth."

George Cantrell came around to look over her shoulder.

"Matching yours?"

"Sounds like it." Cochetta scrolled through the information. She pushed back away from the desk forcing George to step away.

"Any luck with the forensics from the last victim?"

"Not really. They found a hair but no follicle. It was also dyed. That could have come from anyplace. We know the perp moved the bodies from the actual crime scene. BCIP was negative, so no semen present. No signs of penetration. No blood. Except for the hair the body was clean as a whistle."

"If only," George said. "At least a whistle would give us some DNA. Looks like you're in for another trip. Maybe this time you'll have better luck. You want me to assign someone to keep you company?"

"No, I'll contact Company B and ask for someone familiar with the Ft. Worth area."

"Ask for Lou Chapman. He's one of our best."

Cochetta scribbled down the name.

"Well, there's nothing I can do to help this woman now so I'll drive up later in the week. I want to review the files on our victims to see if there's something that was overlooked before I talk to whoever's in charge of the Ft. Worth case." Cochetta ran her fingers through her long salt-and-pepper hair. "Let's hope he'll be able to provide a break in the case."

"You still think the killer is a woman?"

"I know it is. Call it a gut feeling. Anyway, headquarters was notified by the Ft. Worth police department and asked that all the information be forwarded to me immediately. The medical examiner's report says this victim's eyes were also pinned open. That's not a coincidence."

"Why in the hell would someone do that?"

"Same reason they rape or kill. It's a sick world out there." Cochetta spun in her chair to look at the array of photos on the back wall of her office. "As for our victims, I've tracked two of them to lesbian bars near the body dump sites. That's the only thing they have in common so far, besides age and gender. I'm betting we eventually find the third one frequented similar establishments." Cochetta had spent weeks making the lesbian connection.

The photos were of the three mutilated women who had been murdered across the state. The first body discovered in San Antonio, the second in Austin and the last in Houston. Local law enforcement agencies initially failed to make a connection between the ways the bodies were laid out. Once they did, they put politics above public safety and the importance of the victims. Each police department wanted to be the one to solve the cases and make the arrest. Serial killers were big news.

Eventually the governor had no choice but to get involved. He wasn't happy about the adverse publicity. Three young women being brutally murdered with crosses carved on their foreheads provided the press the opportunity for a feeding frenzy, not to mention fodder for his political opponents. No suspects and jurisdictional turf wars weren't good for his re-election campaign. The Rangers were ordered to initiate their own investigations.

The files had been tossed on Cochetta's desk. If a female Ranger solved the cases, all the better. The governor would gain the support of several prominent women's organizations for being progressive by assigning a female to lead the task force.

Cochetta knew as chief investigator, the pressure was on. She wasn't about to screw it up. For her there was more than pride at stake. Picking up an old photo next to a stack of files, Cochetta stared at the two images holding a dark-haired infant.

I won't let you down, Pop. I'm going to be the best Ranger Texas ever had.

†

Cochetta spent the first sixteen years of her life on the Mescalero Apache Reservation in New Mexico, one of the few remaining tribal territories of the Apache people. It was a harsh land—hot, dry, and brutal to anyone foolish enough not to take it seriously. At age three Cochetta received her first lesson on just how cruel it could be. While tending a garden next to their small home her mom was bitten by a Western Diamondback rattlesnake. Elan Lovejoy, her father, was a tribal police officer. On a domestic call, he was more than forty minutes away. By the time he arrived home, Inayat was dead. Cochetta remembered sitting on the ground playing in the dirt. She thought her mother had fallen asleep. Her father had found her curled up next to her Shi ma, the Apache word for mother. She wouldn't wake up.

Life after that became complicated. Elan was a loving father, wanting only the best for his daughter. He taught her the traditions of both of his people, Apache and the white world. Knowing she would have no future if she stayed on the reservation, he spent years agonizing on what to do with her once she entered her teens. As a blossoming, attractive young woman, she would become a target for rogue males who roamed about. Although Cochetta was tough and quite capable of defending herself under most circumstances, she stood no chance against the small bands that prowled around searching for easy prey. Rape and sexual assault was sadly all too common amongst the residents on the reservation. More than once, she had come home from school bruised and bloodied, but never defeated.

The year Cochetta started high school, Elan decided to send her to live with his cousin in Texas. Cochetta was devastated, but also relieved; devastated at leaving behind the land and father she loved; relieved to be out of the dangerous environment. They both knew he couldn't protect her forever.

Sadly, two years later, while investigating an abandoned vehicle on a lonely stretch of highway he was killed in a hit-and-run accident. The driver was never apprehended. Some people believed Elan's death wasn't an accident. As a law enforcement officer, he wasn't very popular among some of the locals.

Cochetta vowed she would catch his murderer no matter how long it took. The only way she could accomplish that was to become a cop herself. Majoring in criminal justice, she received her degree in three and a half years and then applied to the San Antonio police academy. Cochetta was immediately snapped up. It was the springboard she needed to gain the required experience to be accepted into the Texas Ranger program.

†

Cochetta shook her head. Old memories weren't pleasant, especially those that reminded her of her failings. She eventually accepted she would never find out who killed her father. It was a bitter realization, but also almost inspirational. Once Ranger Cochetta Lovejoy was assigned a case, she would do whatever it took to solve it and catch the perpetrator. Now, the memories were just distractions. She needed to concentrate on her present assignment, the brutal murder of three women.

A local San Antonio paper had coined the name "Rapture Killer" after the third murder. The bodies were laid out heads pointing west, feet pointing east. Their hands were bound together in a prayer position. Crosses had been carved on the foreheads. Reporters speculated that the killings were religious based; maybe ritual sacrifices, thus the name. The Rapture signaled Christ's second coming. Wide bruises on the wrists and legs indicated the victims were restrained, but not by handcuffs. The patterns closely matched the leather or nylon restraints used in bondage.

When she was first handed the case, Cochetta carefully studied each victim's file. Then she contacted an FBI profiler hoping to gain more insight into the killer's personality.

Clearly he or she... *She!* Cochetta thought, appeared to be targeting lesbians. The killer was probably in her mid-to-late thirties. Carved crosses and the positioning of the bodies were rituals indicating a strong religious background, probably Protestant or Catholic. There were either sexuality issues or a bad experience that had a lesbian connection.

As a seasoned officer, Cochetta was used to seeing dead bodies. These women, however, were different, and familiar. She thought about an encounter she had several months earlier. While in Houston, she'd met a woman who fit the profiler's description...Kelly. Cochetta would never forget the woman's face or how she herself had almost been trapped into becoming a willing victim. That moment of panic...of weakness. If she hadn't come to her senses, her photo would probably be on someone's wall.

I was probably her first attempt, Cochetta thought once she had put two and two together. Lesbians, restraints, and religion. Kelly had a rosary hanging on the headboard.

After leaving the hotel, the Ranger went back to the bar. Her desire to get laid was gone, replaced by a burning anger. How could she have put herself in that position? After downing a couple of drinks, she felt better, until Kelly showed up again and then left with another woman.

Several beers later, she decided to find out a little more about this *Kelly.* Hoping her position would influence the manager she pressed him for more information about his customer. The manager refused, telling her to get a warrant. Cochetta wasn't about to reveal to a judge that she had allowed herself to be picked up for a one-night stand. Besides, that alone wasn't enough probable cause to prove anything. All she could do was create notes from what she remembered and have a forensic artist create a sketch based on her memory. Fortunately, Cochetta had a very good memory. The drawing was pinned to the wall amongst the pictures of the dead victims.

Chapter 4

Five days after the discovery of the first body in the Stockyards, a second one turned up at Tarantula Train Station. The day was cold, wet, and miserable.

Agnes was not in a good mood. The dismal weather made her whole body ache. She pulled her jacket tighter around her as she stepped away from her car. A gust of wind sent sharp bits of sleet against her exposed skin. Her arthritis was acting up.

God I hate the cold. I need to do something about this crap, she thought, rubbing her hands together to relieve the ache. Ibuprofen no longer calmed the painful flare-ups. *Damn weather!*

The body was shielded from prying eyes by an ambulance and a fire truck. Tarps were strung between them making it impossible for the onlookers to see what was beyond. Rainy days didn't stop gawkers. Agnes angled into the makeshift tent and bumped into Jeff.

"Aren't you just Johnny-on-the-spot! Don't you have a life?" she asked the young detective as she pulled on latex gloves. After spending a transitional period with a training officer in her department, he had been assigned as her partner. Normally, Agnes hated working with newbies. They tended to be overly ambitious or cocky. Jeff was different. He was good, although a bit too enthusiastic, an admirable quality, but annoying at times.

"Not since my girlfriend dumped me. Besides, when dispatch calls, I come." Jeff shrugged.

"That's probably why you got dumped."

Ignoring the comment Jeff pointed to the body on the ground.

"Looks familiar, huh?"

"Damn it!" Agnes growled when she saw the body's position and the arrangement of the woman's limbs. "We have a serial killer on our hands."

"Two bodies does not a serial killer make, Elliott," Jeff protested.

Agnes groped her notepad from her jacket pocket, surprised the young detective hadn't already made the connection between the Ft. Worth murders and three others across the state.

You need to do your homework a little better, Agnes thought. *Little mistakes lead to bigger ones.* She decided to teach him a lesson.

"I bet you twenty we have another victim in a few days if we don't catch the killer before then."

Jeff considered the bet.

"Let's hope we catch him, but just in case, how many is a few?"

"Five."

"Make it a fifty and you're on."

Agnes barely contained a smug smile. The thought of more victims bothered her but she knew it was inevitable. Serial killers weren't easy to catch and didn't just stop. Crouching, she examined the arms and legs. "Same ligature marks on the wrists and ankles. Same positioning of the hands and body. This is the Rapture Killer's work. You sure you don't want to back out of the bet?"

"Nope! We could have a whacko that picked up two girls and took his time killing them. Besides I could use the extra bucks."

Agnes looked up at him in disbelief.

"You can't really believe that whacko bullshit."

"It's possible and it's a reasonable theory."

"Give me a break!" Agnes shook her head. *You're going to deserve losing this one.*

The victim was in her early twenties with dark brown hair. The blue-gray film of death covered her lifeless eyes as they stared upward. Agnes pulled her camera out of her jacket pocket and snapped several pictures. The investigation of the first victim had turned up little. She was still a Jane Doe. Hopefully they would have better luck with this one. Noticing a tattoo on the woman's arm, she snapped two shots.

"She might be gay."

Jeff crouched next to Agnes and lifted the arm gently to get a better look at the rainbow-colored Chinese character.

"Lesbians aren't the only ones with colorful tattoos. I wonder what that means."

"Woman. And the colors represent a rainbow," Agnes explained.

"Okay, I get the rainbow thing, but you know it says 'woman' how?" Jeff questioned as he lowered the limb back to its original position.

"I've seen it before. The rest you can chalk up to intuition," Agnes answered, hoping to end the line of questioning.

"Fair enough," Jeff said with a shrug.

They worked silently, inventorying the body before checking with the CSI unit who was scanning the area for additional evidence. Agnes finally closed her notepad three hours later and headed back to the station.

✝

The next day found Agnes at the Tarrant County Medical Examiner's office. Autopsies were a necessity but she deplored the thought of cutting open bodies. The coroner's office had an indescribable smell—a strange mixture of disinfectant and decay—the kind of smell that was impossible to forget. Then there were the technicians…quirky, geeky people who got off on identifying weird bugs or worms in dead people's skulls or any place else they might be hiding.

Agnes managed a slight smile as she approached one of the junior medical examiners who was standing near a partially decapitated body. She wore a protective plastic shield over her face and held a small buzzing saw in her hand. The woman gave her a friendly smile.

"I'm done here, Robby. I think I'll get a bite to eat," she called out, looking past Agnes to a man standing several tables away. *Geez!* Agnes thought, *can you be any creepier?* Moving on to another table where her Jane Doe No. 1 lay with a white sheet covering her from ankles to neck, she averted her eyes. Jane Doe didn't have a name but the detective felt a connection to the victim.

The senior medical examiner was sitting in his office, glancing through some paperwork. Agnes tapped on the window.

"Elliott," he said, not looking up. "What took you so long? You're normally here hours after we get a body…not days."

"Hey, Pete. Yeah, heavy workload these days and two of our guys are out sick." If Agnes had to name her favorite coroner it was Pete Winsfield. He was in his early fifties, notoriously cranky, and appeared to dislike people. When it came down to business, though, he was among the very best in his field. "Got anything new to tell me?"

"Probably not, or at least not much. First victim, obviously female, mid-twenties. We're running her prints. If she's been in the system or a state employee, we'll get a hit soon. Other than being dead she was quite healthy." Agnes *tsked* Pete for being glib but he ignored it and continued with his report. "Come with me." The medical examiner walked toward the refrigeration storage units. Opening one door, he slid the tray out and pulled back a sheet exposing the upper half of the corpse. "Pretty girl," he said, shaking his head. "Cause of death, suffocation. She definitely struggled against her bonds causing extensive trauma to the tissues on her wrists and ankles. I removed leather fibers imbedded in the wounds on the wrists. I suspect they are like the ones commonly used in bondage."

Agnes could feel her cheeks growing warm and was thankful that Pete was preoccupied with the body.

"Her hands were posed postmortem, tied together with a sixteen-inch length of nylon cord. No trace matter on it. She was thoroughly washed. No particulates under the nails. No foreign DNA anywhere on the body. The cross carved on her forehead appears postmortem, possibly an afterthought."

"Just what we need, an OCD religious freak."

Pete pulled a portable magnifying glass/light combo around and settled it over the woman's open eyes.

"This is the interesting thing." He focused the magnifier and motioned for Agnes to come closer. "See those small silver dots?"

Leaning closer to the lens, Agnes nodded.

"What are they?"

"Pins. Her eyelids were pinned open. I decided not to remove them until after showing them to you. It's probably the most critical part of the killer's MO. A personal signature, so to speak."

"Yeah, but why do that?" Agnes thought aloud. "And what about the other victim?"

Pete slid the body back into refrigeration and crossed to another table. Drawing the sheet back he leaned over to point at a similar silver dot.

"Same thing. Maybe the killer wants the victims to see who's killing them. If they were alive when this was done, it had to be excruciating. The ligature marks are similar. Pinned eyelids. A cross carved onto the forehead, again postmortem. Death is probably by suffocation. I can't be sure until I complete the autopsy." Pete spread the sheet back over the body of the latest Jane Doe. "I have photos for you. This young woman might have a connection to the gay community. I've seen that tattoo before. You remember a few years ago when three lesbians were assaulted by that Randolph fellow? One of them had the same tattoo. Well, that's about it until we get the lab work and fingerprint reports. I sure hope you get this guy soon."

Agnes accepted the envelope holding more than a dozen photos.

"So do I, Pete. We're certainly going to do our best."

"You always do." Pete smiled at her. "Well, I guess I'd better get back to work. These bodies won't take care of themselves. I'll be glad when this flu epidemic is over. Between being shorthanded and rash of murders, we're barely keeping up with the workload. Later, Detective. Stay safe out there." Turning Pete hailed one of his assistants to follow him.

Chapter 5

Cochetta pulled her Stetson down to shade her eyes. The glare of the afternoon sun reflected off the glass skyscrapers in downtown Ft. Worth. It was a chilly forty-five degrees. Reluctantly she left the warm interior of her Bronco. Not familiar with the city, Cochetta glanced at the map in her hand. She was two hours late for her meeting. Hopefully, the department's lead investigator was still at PD. Two victims, in less than a week, in the same town didn't fit the profile of her other cases, but the details of the murders did.

After locating the police station, she was informed by the desk sergeant that the detectives were out on a call, another murder, a place called Trinity River.

✝

Rounding a corner, Cochetta sighed with relief when she saw the throng of police cars parked along a stretch of river. According to the desk sergeant, she was looking for Lt. Kelly Elliott.

I hope he isn't an asshole.

She had run into her fair share during her career. People skills were not her forté, although Cochetta could be charming when it called for it. Assholes, however, really tested her patience, especially local police officers who had jurisdiction issues.

Sliding out of her truck, she zipped up her coat. The crime scene was surrounded by yellow tape warning bystanders to stay back. Cochetta flashed her badge at the policeman assigned to keep the crowd at bay.

"Sorry, miss," the officer said. "I need to see an ID too."

"I'm looking for Lt. Elliott," Cochetta said, complying with the request. The policeman motioned her toward the river.

"The detectives are down there. Look for the redhead with the attitude."

Just what I need. A local with an attitude.

The sound of an angry voice told her she was heading in the right direction. Someone was clearly dressing down a visibly shaken officer.

"In what manual did you read that you should touch a body before detectives arrive?"

"I'm sorry, Lieutenant. I wasn't thinking—"

"You're damn right you weren't! Get out of my sight! And in the future, you wait, you preserve, and you don't touch, understand?"

Cochetta watched the officer sulk off, and then looked back at the woman who had been reprimanding him. Her heart jumped in her chest.

"Kelly?"

†

Startled at hearing her name, Agnes looked up. Few people called her that; mostly the women she had interacted with on a more personal level. Several feet away stood the woman from the bar in Houston.

"Crap!" she muttered. *This isn't good.*

"Hey, Elliott!" Donny called from a short distance away.

Agnes pulled her eyes away from Cochise to look at the photographer.

"What?" she yelled back.

"How far do you want me to go?" Donny lifted his arms away from his sides like a little kid waiting for directions. "I'm finished over here."

Agnes closed her eyes and shook her head then looked back at the man.

"Just shoot the entire area, a hundred yards on each side and all the way to the street!" She carefully stepped around the dead woman on the grass and walked over to Cochise. "What the hell are you doing here?"

"I am Sgt. Cochetta Lovejoy of the Texas Rangers. The bigger question is who you are? What's your full name, Lt. Elliott?" Cochetta hissed between clenched teeth.

"Excuse me, Sgt. Lovejoy. I doubt if you talk to your senior officers like this. I'll be damned if you're going to use that tone on me."

†

Cochetta was at a loss. Here stood her number one suspect for three murders, possibly six now, and she was a cop.

"My apologies, *Lieutenant*," Cochetta replied, her voice tinged with sarcasm. "I need your name for my report."

25

Agnes's eyes stared coldly at the Ranger for several seconds.

"Lt. Agnes Kelly-Elliott. That's with a hyphen. I asked why you are here, Sergeant."

"Convenient," Cochetta muttered to herself as she turned away from the detective to look at the river. "Your three victims are of special interest to me."

"Why?"

The question seemed genuine. Cochetta turned around and looked directly into those bright green eyes she remembered so well.

"You have three bodies. I have three bodies." She paid close attention to Agnes's reaction. There was a hint of surprise.

"You're investigating the Rapture Killer?" Agnes ran her hands through her hair. "How long have you been on the case?"

"Long enough to have a good idea who I'm looking for," Cochetta said. Agnes gave her a curious look. *So you want to play games,* the Ranger thought. She decided to go along with it…for now. "I was assigned the case a few months ago. The local authorities weren't getting along. Politics as usual."

"Local authorities?"

"Yeah! San Antonio, Austin, and Houston. But you know that, don't you?" When Agnes frowned Cochetta smirked. "You did say you read the reports. Surely you're aware of the murder sites."

✝

Agnes walked about ten paces away from the body that lay on the ground, and the accusatory eyes of Ranger Lovejoy. *What the hell's your problem, lady?* she thought. Okay, so their first encounter wasn't exactly pleasant. The woman was a bit too overreactive, not exactly a good trait for a law enforcement officer. Now, here she was displaying an arrogance Agnes found even more irritating along with her posture, her tone, her insinuation. Spinning angrily, she glared at Cochise-Cochetta.

"Do you have a problem with me, Ranger Lovejoy?"

"Problem? Not at all! In fact, I think you're about to help me solve this case."

"Meaning what?"

"I think you know, Lieutenant Kelly-Elliott. I think you know exactly what I mean."

Agnes stiffened.

"You aren't seriously inferring that I have something to do with these murders, are you?"

Cochetta cocked her head slightly.

"And if I am? It wouldn't be the first time a cop crossed the line…and being a detective is the perfect cover."

"Do you always jump to conclusions so quickly?"

"When I have enough evidence, and I believe I do."

"Well then, I'm sure you won't mind sharing it," Agnes said. When Cochise just stared at her Agnes's eyebrows shot upward. "Unless you're bluffing and this is really about something else."

"Like what?" Cochetta crossed her arms nonchalantly.

Body language, Agnes thought, *it's always about body language.* The Ranger's stance was insultingly casual.

"Like what happened in Houston?" she replied, crossing her own arms. *I can play this game too.* "I really scared you, didn't I?"

Cochetta's eyes flashed with anger.

That got your attention! Agnes thought.

"Dream on, Detective. You don't have what it takes to scare me. And we both know this isn't about me. It's about five murders, maybe six. You fit an FBI profiler's description of the killer. I don't think that's a coincidence."

"Really? He or she told you a female police officer who happens to pick up female police officers for sex is the killer? I know they're good but no one's that good. Did you happen to mention our encounter?" Agnes shook her head, answering her own question. "No, you wouldn't. That wouldn't go down well with the department, would it?"

The Ranger's arms unfolded and dropped to her side.

"Don't try to turn this around. You have the means and I'm betting the motive. Tell me," she said, "are you out or still hiding in the closet?"

Agnes stiffened, straightening to her full five foot eight height.

"You're crazy! What happened between us has nothing to do with this and you know it. I said I was sorry. Get over it! Besides, you're a big girl. You wanted the same thing I did."

An almost cruel smile appeared on the Ranger's face.

"I don't think so. You wanted control, remember? When I didn't give it to you, you panicked. Was I to be your first victim or just practice?"

Agnes shook her head.

"Your memory is a little lacking, Ranger. **I had control**. You're the one who got scared. You practically threw me on the floor with that wild bucking. Lucky for you I wasn't the killer or a sex predator. I could have taken you right then and there."

"Over my dead body," Cochetta hissed.

Smiling, Agnes let her body relax.

"Exactly. But it wasn't and I'm not, which is why you're standing here right acting like some rookie. Now if you don't mind I have work to do. I don't have time for this bullshit. If you'll excuse me—"

"Make time!" Cochetta ordered, her voice ice cold from barely controlled anger. "Because I sure as hell am going to and you are my prime suspect. I intend to expose you for what you are. A perverted, sadistic killer."

"I don't take orders from you, Lovejoy, so back off! You know, I thought Texas Rangers were supposed to be the cream of the crop. Professionals. How you qualified is beyond me. You obviously need a refresher course in investigation, Ranger. Even rookies know not to reveal their hand to a suspect."

"Rookies don't have my experience, and I'm rarely wrong."

"Fuck you!" Agnes walked away, up the riverbank toward her car. "Donny, I've done everything I need to," she called out to the photographer. "Ranger Lovejoy, here, seems to have a special interest in this case so she might have a few questions. Tell her what we know so far and make sure she reciprocates. Maybe they have something that will help us out."

This entire situation had just become surreal. Agnes suddenly stopped and rubbed her forehead with her right palm. *That idiot actually thinks I'm the Rapture Killer.* It made no sense. The woman couldn't be that stupid or vindictive over the Houston debacle. Still, if she was and carried out her threat, life was going to become hell very quickly. *Everyone will know! My friends, my family. They'll disown me.* Then there was the department. She wasn't doing anything illegal but the department didn't like scandals. She glanced back at the Ranger. *I need to think...to...to what? I can't undo what's been done and I sure can't make my past go away.*

†

Cochetta watched the detective walk away. If she was wrong...but she knew she wasn't. Perhaps Kelly was right, though. Maybe she had shown her hand too soon. There certainly wasn't enough evidence for a conviction, possibly not even for a warrant. She would need to convince one of the local judges otherwise. Cochetta was confident Kelly's home would produce what she needed to make an arrest. The victims had been restrained. Kelly was into bondage. She was also into women. Thinking back to her first encounter with the detective, the Ranger remembered the rosary hanging on the headboard. Only a religious person would carry such a significant icon with them for casual sex.

More like a religious nut!

Pulling a small notebook from her shirt pocket she flipped through several pages before locating the contact information she needed. One particular judge had come to mind. Ambitious, the woman had cooperated with Cochetta on some previous cases. A few times the probable cause had been weak but she didn't seem to mind signing the search warrants. Every defendant had been convicted. The judge was in her glory. Her reputation for toughness enhanced her career and she was now being considered for an appellate position.

Kelly's the perpetrator! And I just let her know. If she decides to run…shit!

Cochetta jogged up the hill to her Bronco ignoring Donny's questioning call to her. Speeding away from the murder site, she ended up five cars behind Agnes. The distance provided good cover but put her at a disadvantage. After running two red lights, the impromptu chase ended at a church in the heart of downtown Ft. Worth. Cochetta parked and watched the detective enter St. Patrick's Cathedral. At first it seemed like an odd place to run off to, especially for a serial killer. Then she thought about the bodies. The hands were always arranged in a prayer position. Now it all made sense. The profiler and the reporters were right. This was about the Rapture. Kelly wanted her victims to see Christ's arrival.

She probably thinks God's going to grant her redemption or something.

Slowly pushing on the heavy wooden church door, Cochetta entered a small foyer that opened into a room filled with pews. Several people were scattered about, their heads lowered in silent prayer. It took her a few seconds to locate Kelly. Backing up, she quietly retraced her steps to the outside and flipped open her cell phone. A few minutes later she slid into a pew a few rows behind the kneeling woman.

Kelly knelt steadily on the prayer bench for almost an hour, only moving to wipe her eyes or nose. Obviously distressed, she seemed to be nearing a breaking point. That meant she would begin to make mistakes. Cochetta intended on being around when that happened.

A tap on the Ranger's shoulder startled her. Behind her stood Lou Chapman, the local Ranger assigned to assist her in the investigation.

Motioning for him to go back out she glanced one more time at the detective. She hadn't moved.

✝

"What took you so long?" Cochetta asked.

"I was talking with the captain when you called. Captain tops sergeant," Lou said. "What's up?"

She quickly filled him in on the current situation.

"You really think she's the killer?" he asked, sounding a bit skeptical.

"I wouldn't be here if I didn't. She fits the profile. Young, religious, closeted lesbian. As a cop she can—"

"Lesbian? And how do you know that?"

"I just know. I wouldn't be wasting my time here if I wasn't sure."

"If you say so," Lou replied skeptically.

"Call it gut instinct if you want, Lou, but she's the killer. I'll stake my badge on it," Cochetta said.

Lou shrugged.

"Your head, not mine. I'll play along for now. You haven't been wrong yet when it comes to finding the bad guys. A lot of women fit that description, though. Hell, we're not even sure the killer's a woman. The profiler said it could be either. We need more evidence than we have, and no one's going to convict her because she's a closeted lesbian."

"By the time I finish with her she'll convict herself."

Lou gave Cochetta a curious look.

"This sounds almost personal. Do you know her?"

Stiffening, Cochetta glared at Lou.

"That's a stupid question."

Throwing up both hands Lou took a step backward.

"Sorry. What do you want me to do?"

"Keep an eye on her. I'm going to talk with a judge and then the detective's supervisor. If I can get a record of her days off, I'm betting it will confirm what I suspect. There's not a doubt in my mind that I'll find my proof in her house. I want to put an end to these killings."

"Listen, Cochetta, I'm as anxious to get this killer as you are but you're going to have to come up with something big. Your suspicions won't cut it in court."

"Just do it, Lou. I'll get the proof."

30

Chapter 6

Agnes drove to the only place that offered her peace. She needed to calm down, figure a way out of this situation. It was hard to believe the Ranger was being vindictive when nothing had actually happened, but why else would she be doing this? If Lovejoy made a stink the publicity alone would ruin Agnes's reputation and career, possibly even Cochetta's. The Ranger would be exposing herself to the same type of scrutiny. Of course if she was already out of the closet...

This can't be happening. I'll lose everything...my family, my friends. They'll never accept or understand why I do it.

Then there was the matter of being a murder suspect. The Ranger could probably put together enough circumstantial evidence to present a weak case, but the damage would be done. The press would run wild with the news until Agnes cleared herself. The detective's hands balled into fists.

Why are you doing this? I'm not perfect. I know what I'm doing is wrong but I try to make up for it every day. Tears streamed down her cheeks as she stared up at the statue of Christ. Confused and exhausted Agnes leaned back into the pew. Her feet tingled from the awkwardness of kneeling. When she glanced at her watch, she gasped. Over two hours had passed since she arrived at the church. *I need to talk to the captain.*

Sliding from her seat, she hurried down the long carpeted aisle and out the door. A cold wind caught her by surprise. Agnes shivered as she trudged toward her car. Had she bothered to look around, she would have seen the tall man following a short distance behind her, before rushing to his own vehicle.

✝

Dusk was settling as she pulled into the station parking lot. The graying sky matched her somber mood. Pushing open the door she noticed the desk sergeant picking up his phone as soon as he saw her. This evening there was no friendly wave, no comfortable banter between comrades when she passed his station. Her stomach churned. Agnes dashed into the women's bathroom barely making it to the toilet before wrenching violently. Nothing came up. The dry heaves continued for several minutes. Her head felt like it was about to split in two. Eventually her stomach ceased rebelling. Exhausted, Agnes stumbled to the sink to rinse out her mouth. Staring at the mirror she was mesmerized by the pale reflection with the haunted eyes. *You're weak,* Agnes accused. The pathetic image said nothing.

"Lt. Kelly-Elliott?"

Kelly turned to a young female officer standing in the doorway.

"Yes…yes?"

"Captain Gonzales wants to speak with you in Interview Room Two."

"I'll be right there."

The woman looked apologetic.

"I'm supposed to escort you."

The officer was new to the force. Agnes could see she was uncomfortable, even slightly nervous.

"I suppose he wants you to deliver me without my gun." Agnes reached toward her shoulder holster.

"Please don't do that, Lieutenant," the officer said, pointing her own firearm at Agnes. "Put your hands up."

Agnes slowly raised her hands.

"I was only going to hand it to you. Do your job, officer," she said and waited while the cop removed her weapon.

"Sorry, ma'am, but I'm just following orders. Let's go."

✝

Inside the interrogation room was an empty plastic chair facing a table. Three people sat on the opposite side, Jeff Roberts, Captain Michael Gonzales, and Ranger Lovejoy. Agnes's escort gave the captain the firearm and then left.

"Do I need an attorney?" Agnes asked, taking the empty seat. Resting her forearms on the table, she interlaced her fingers and looked pointedly at Captain Gonzales. Her initial panic had subsided. Now all she felt was an eerie calmness.

"Agnes, Ranger Lovejoy is making some pretty serious allegations about you. Are you guilty?" Gonzales asked as he removed the clip from the gun.

"Of what?"

Jeff leaned forward.

"This isn't a game, Agnes. The captain asked me here because I'm your partner. He thought you might feel better if—"

Agnes silenced him with a look of total disgust before looking back at her supervisor.

"Am I being charged with something?"

"Nothing has been filed."

"Then why am I here?"

"We have some questions that need to be answered," Captain Gonzales said.

"Need? That makes it sound like I should at least have a union rep here."

Gonzales looked at Ranger Lovejoy and then back at his detective.

"Listen, I'd like this straightened out as quickly as possible before something gets blown out of proportion. Ranger Lovejoy says you're involved with these recent murders. I say she's full of shit! If you'll answer a few questions we can clear this up quickly, she can get the hell out of here, and everyone else can get back to work."

"I see. Whatever she told you must be pretty compelling for things to have gotten this far. What did she say to make you believe her?"

"I don't believe her. As far as I'm concerned this is pure bullshit. Unfortunately, I'm not at liberty to say what she said," Captain Gonzales replied, glancing uncomfortably down at his hands, which were now tightly clasped and resting on the table.

"I guess this interview is over then. There's no way I'm answering anything until someone tells me what I'm being accused of and what the evidence is. I'd like to get back to work now. There's a killer out there."

Agnes jumped in her chair when Cochetta Lovejoy's hand crashed down on the tabletop.

"You're not going anywhere!"

Gonzales put a restraining hand on the Ranger's shoulder.

"Ranger Lovejoy, I remind you I'm in charge. Your presence here is a courtesy, so please sit down and shut up." Reluctantly Cochetta settled back onto her chair. "Look, Agnes," Gonzales said, "let's just talk about this for a bit. See if we can figure out what's going on."

Agnes took a deep breath and exhaled slowly.

"What exactly do you want to know?"

"Is she right about you?" Jeff asked.

Agnes slowly turned her gaze, making contact with her partner's eyes.

"That depends on what she told you. No one's bothered to tell me why I'm here?"

"Your game is over, Detective. Why drag this out anymore?" Ranger Lovejoy growled. "I know you're the Rapture Killer. You fit the profile. You're a lesbian and into bondage. Your off-duty time matches the dates of the murdered women here in Ft. Worth. You were also in San Antonio when that murder occurred. Every victim was meticulously cleaned and staged at a secondary site. Your expertise in law enforcement would account for the lack of forensic evidence. Your religious belief explains why the bodies were positioned the way they were. As a cop you easily gained each victim's trust so you could practice your perversions."

"That's the third time you've referred to me in that manner," Agnes said, her voice cold with anger. Her partner and the captain's eyes shifted from Agnes's face to the Ranger's, but neither said anything. "Your evidence is bullshit and you know it. As for my religious beliefs, you don't know a thing about that. The off-duty roster times match two-thirds of this department's force and every other law enforcement agency in the state. And my sexuality is no one's business, especially not yours. Now, I really would like to speak to my union rep."

The Ranger leaned forward menacingly. Smiling smugly she pointed her right index finger at Agnes.

"I know more about you than you think, Elliott! You're Catholic. You believe in the Rapture. You're clearly a closeted lesbian and once we finish combing through your house I'm sure we'll have all the proof we need to charge you with these murders."

"You have no right—"

"Tell that to Judge Elroy. She's convinced enough of your guilt to sign the warrant."

"Based on what? I want my union rep," Agnes demanded.

"Do you think the union's going to back a serial killer?"

"Ranger," Captain Gonzales interrupted in a tone that couldn't be ignored. "This interview is over. Detective Kelly-Elliott has asked for a rep. The questioning stops now."

"Fine! By all means call them, Captain. I want to make sure everything is by the book. Don't be surprised if they refuse to send someone over, though. Defending someone like her wouldn't be good for their public image. In the meantime, she's to be held here while the warrant is being executed."

"Am I under arrest?" Agnes demanded, jumping to her feet. "Because if this meeting was just a ruse to gain time to search my place—"

"Let's just say you're being detained until we can get this straightened out," Captain Gonzales said. "It shouldn't take long. I can't imagine anything showing up in the search."

Agnes closed her eyes and sank back down into her chair.

Right! I can be stuck here for 72 hours if they want. And you definitely can't imagine what they're going to find in my house.

The three officers left without saying anything else. Agnes sat silently, trying to relax as much as she could under the circumstances. As a detective she was well aware of how the game was played.

✝

Time passed agonizingly slowly. After nearly three hours the door opened again.

"God damn it, Aggie. What the hell have you gotten yourself into?"

Her ex, Griff, sank down across from her.

"I haven't done anything."

"They're saying you're queer." He scrunched up his face. "Is that true?"

"News does travel fast, doesn't it? We're divorced, Griff. My lifestyle isn't any of your business."

Shaking his head, he glared angrily at her.

"Maybe not now, but if you were fucking women while we—"

"Were married? No, I left that up to you," Agnes spat back. "Why the fuck are you here?"

"Jeff called me and said you were in trouble. I couldn't believe what he told me. I came to hear it from you."

"Hear what? I'm being accused of murder and you want to know if I'm queer? Did it bruise your ego? Being a lesbian isn't illegal and it isn't about your manhood."

"I don't give a rat's ass about your personal preferences now, but you could have been honest with me back then." Griff pounded the tabletop. "Damn it, Aggie, they found a pile of shit in your house. Kinky shit! Jeff said they have enough probable cause to charge you." He shook his head and looked at the scarred table surface.

"Jeff seems to say a lot. Be sure to thank him for me."

"He only wants to help."

"Right! I could tell when he was in here. He thinks I'm as guilty as that Ranger does. Look at me, Griff. Do you really think I'm a killer?"

Griff met her gaze and held it.

35

"What about the other stuff, the dates and that stuff they found in your home?"

"Coincidence. Nothing more. You have to believe me."

"What do I tell the kids? And your folks?" Griff leaned forward, resting his arms on the tabletop. "What the hell am I going to tell them?"

"The truth! I didn't do this. Hell, let them find out when the news comes out in the morning. I don't care." Agnes felt defeated. She was going to be outed and accused of being a killer. For some reason the outing seemed more devastating than the latter.

Griff sat back in his chair and ran his hands through his thick black hair.

"This is all fucked up." He stood and moved toward the door.

"Griff," Agnes called softly and was relieved when he stopped with his hand on the doorknob. He turned back toward her and waited to hear what she would say. "I didn't kill those women."

Griff pressed his lips into a thin line and then nodded.

"I believe you. Hang in there. Don't tell the bastards a thing. You know better than anyone how this system works."

Agnes felt the tears well up in her eyes.

"I won't…and…thanks." She watched him go.

It was another five hours before someone else came into the room to see if she needed to use the restroom. Agnes was escorted to the bathroom and back to the interview room. Jeff, Captain Gonzales, and Ranger Lovejoy were back in their seats when she returned.

"Do you need something to drink?" Captain Gonzales asked.

"No." She had taken a few swallows of water from the faucet when she was in the restroom.

"Do you want to make a statement before we make the announcement?" Lovejoy asked.

Agnes looked perplexed about the question.

"To the press," the Ranger clarified.

Agnes shook her head.

"You're already planning a press release? I haven't even been charged. What's the rush?"

As if on cue the door swung open and a man that wasn't familiar to Agnes dropped a thick pile of paper on the table in front of Ranger Lovejoy. He gave Agnes a look of pure disgust before he exited.

Agnes sat back in her chair while the Ranger looked over the pages in front of her.

"Wrong, *Miss* Elliott." The emphasis on 'Miss' didn't escape Agnes. "You're being charged with murder. You have the right to remain silent, you have the right to an attorney…"

"I know my rights. I'm not saying anything else without one."

Jeff and Captain Gonzales got up from their seats.

"I'll check on the attorney," Jeff said. "Are you coming, Ranger?"

"Not yet and don't worry, I'm not going to ask her any more questions." Once they were gone, Cochetta turned her attention back to Agnes. "It's too bad you don't want to cooperate. This would be a lot easier on you. We have enough evidence for the State to make a good solid case. Let's see. San Antonio, September 14th." Cochetta looked up at Agnes "You were at the Marriott two days, according to your credit card. We found your next victim three days after your stay at the Victoria Super 8. Now we have three more murders around Ft. Worth. Coincidence? That's not a question, Kelly, just an observation."

"How do you account for the others?" Agnes asked, unable to suppress her curiosity.

"I'll figure those out. We haven't put together all the details of your travels yet but we will."

"This is ridiculous," Agnes said angrily. "I'm sorry I scared you when we met in Houston but that's no reason to—"

"You're a sadistic pervert. That's the only reason I need," Cochetta said, cutting Agnes off.

"I want a lawyer, now."

Cochetta sat back in her chair.

"Fine. Call him," she said, holding out her cell phone.

Agnes panicked.

"I…I don't have one."

"Not my problem, but I suggest you call someone quickly because you're on your way to county lockup."

Agnes paled.

"You can't send me to county just like that."

"Sure I can." She tapped the pile of papers. "That's where criminals…oh excuse me…alleged criminals go. There's plenty of evidence to substantiate the charge! Now are you going to make that call or not?"

"I'm not using your phone to make my call," Agnes said, stalling for time. "Get mine."

Cochetta snapped her fingers at the mirror and motioned toward Agnes. The cell phone was brought in several minutes later. Not knowing who to call Agnes finally settled on Griff, who told her not to worry, and especially not to cause any trouble with the Ranger. Unfortunately, it was going to take him some time to locate a decent attorney able to defend her. And then there was the cost. Good defense attorneys didn't come cheap.

"How long before your attorney gets here?" Cochetta asked.

"I don't know."

"Well, we're not staying here all night."

"I'm not going anywhere. I'm sure Captain—"

"Your captain no longer has any say in this matter."

"You can't—"

"I can and I'm going to. And don't think you'll get special treatment because you're a cop. As of now this is a state case. Your department no longer has jurisdiction. Maybe after a little time in lockup you'll be more cooperative." Cochetta's smug smile was more than Agnes could stand. Jumping up, she slammed both hands on the table, barely controlling her temper.

"My life wouldn't be worth a damn if you put me in jail."

"All the more reason to tell me what I want now," Cochetta said calmly. "No? Well, you will soon enough." Turning she left the room.

Minutes later the Ranger, Agnes's captain and two uniformed officers entered the room. Her badge and ID were seized along with her shoulder holster. She was pushed against a wall and searched, her pockets turned inside out. The money clip, loose change, and rosary hit the tabletop behind her. Her watch and ring, a gift from her grandmother, were removed. Jeff reread the Miranda rights while an officer handcuffed her.

They're really covering their bases, Agnes thought.

She had done this hundreds of times, stripping suspects of their property, their individuality, their dignity and then sending them to a cell to await justice. Now that the table was turned she felt as violated as they must have felt.

Chapter 7

Cochetta sat quietly as she watched the Ft. Worth officers arrest one of their own. She felt nothing but elation as the cuffs clicked into place. Agnes Kelly-Elliott was spun to face her one last time before being taken away for booking. Cochetta didn't believe she had ever seen such a look of utter despair in her entire life. She reached out and picked up the rosary lying amongst the small pile of personal effects and bounced it in her palm.

"I think your God has abandoned you."

"At least that's one thing we may agree on," Agnes answered with a piercing gaze. "You keep it, Ranger Lovejoy. Consider it a memento. Maybe it'll bring you comfort when the next victim turns up." Agnes was pushed from behind and out the door.

†

Captain Gonzales had had enough for one day. He pointed to the empty chair on the other side of the table after Agnes was taken away.

"I don't like this, Ranger Lovejoy. That woman is a fine cop. One of the best detectives I've ever had. If you're wrong—"

"Then I'll be the first to kiss her ass," Cochetta said as she stood. "But I'm not mistaken. We have plenty of corroborating evidence. A few days in lockup and she'll confess. Cops don't do well in the county's general population."

"You can't do that!" he objected. "All cops get isolation for their own protection. She's still innocent un—"

"She's guilty," Cochetta interrupted. "Elliott's no longer your responsibility, Captain. She's state property now."

"Property! You know, Ranger, for some reason this sounds a little too personal. Do you know Lieutenant Kelly-Elliott from somewhere else?"

"I'm just doing my job. Not any different than you. I understand that you want to look after your officer. I'd like to think my supervisor would do the same for me but then I'm not a murderer. Your potential inability to be objective is the reason the state has decided to take over this case. Then, of course, there's the public perception of a possible cover-up. Just be grateful we caught her before any more murders were committed. Your department certainly is."

"You mean the higher-ups. I'm not convinced." Gonzales shook his head sadly. He had done his job but didn't have to like it. Unfortunately police politics always trumped the individual. When Ranger Lovejoy first approached him about Agnes, he completely rejected her theory. His supervisor, however, had received a call from the Ranger's division commander. Instead of investigating the assertion, the department caved, more than willing to sacrifice one of its own rather than take a lot of heat for doing the right thing. Gonzales was ordered to cooperate with the Ranger.

The captain picked up Agnes's personal effects and silently walked out of the room without looking back. He didn't like Lovejoy or her tactics.

Chapter 8

Mary Sutton walked into the detectives' room, feeling instantly uneasy with the number of unfamiliar people milling about. She wove her way between the cliques of excitedly chatting groups to her desk. Her chair was occupied by a man wearing a press badge.

Great! Fucking idiot probably thinks it's another right the press is entitled to.

He was talking rapidly into the phone, his feet propped up on her desk.

"Excuse me. Would you mind getting your feet off my desk?" she asked. When he continued his banter on the phone, Mary shoved his feet. Then she reached over and pushed another phone line button, disconnecting the call. She didn't tolerate rudeness, especially when it came to being ignored.

"Hey! I was talking." The reporter shook the receiver at her.

"On my phone, at my desk. Did you ask me if you could use it?"

"You weren't around."

"Well, I'm here now. Get out of my chair. I have work to do," Mary said. The reporter stood and tried, unsuccessfully, to match Mary's height. When that didn't work he puffed out his chest and held up his press card.

"See this! You don't want to piss me off, lady. I can make your life miserable. A few words from me and Internal Affairs Division will be breathing down your neck."

Mary looked unconcernedly at the reporter

"Why don't you just go do that? Perhaps you should start with my supervisor first. You know, for the sake of press relations. His name is Captain Gonzales and he's right down the hall. In the meantime I'll be right here…" she scooted by him to her chair. "…sitting at **my** desk. I promise not to move unless I get a call." She didn't give him a second glance as her phone rang. "Detective Sutton, Homicide."

A commotion erupted down the hall causing her to scowl as she pressed the receiver closer to her ear to hear what the person on the other end wanted. It was a reporter for the *Dallas Morning News*. She wanted information about the arrest of Lt. Kelly-Elliott who had been charged for the Rapture Killer murders. Mary's heart fluttered almost painfully in her chest.

"No comment," she said, slamming the phone down. *What the hell!* The racket down the hall was getting louder. Mary went to investigate but was unable to push through a large crowd blocking the hallway. She finally settled on using her height and tiptoes to look over the heads of the people in front of her.

Jeff Roberts was on one side of Agnes holding her arm just above the elbow. Agnes looked distraught but in control of herself. Two uniformed officers followed closely behind.

Mary hurriedly backtracked through the detectives' room and down another hall that led to the police parking lot. Her long strides quickly carried her across the cracked asphalt. The cool air filled her lungs with every deep breath she took. Turning a corner she moved toward the front of the police station, arriving in time to see Agnes pushed into a waiting cruiser. Jogging up to the vehicle, Mary slapped her hands on the glass of the rear window. Agnes turned to look at her, the despair unforgettable. Before Mary could say anything, the car pulled away, leaving her to stare helplessly at the disappearing red taillights. Mary glanced around searching for anyone who could tell her what was happening. Jeff Roberts stood several feet away his gaze locked on the departing cruiser. He looked like a lost little boy.

"Jeff, what's going on?"

"She's the Rapture killer."

Mary walked next to him as he headed back inside.

"Who is? Agnes?"

Jeff nodded.

"I didn't believe it at first. Then I saw the evidence. It's very convincing." He pushed through the station's doors.

"Bullshit! This is Agnes we're talking about. Straight and narrow, Agnes."

Jeff laughed, though it held no humor.

"Funny thing about that. Our straight and narrow Agnes is queer and kinky. She likes to tie her victims up and kills them when she's done."

Mary's head shook back and forth.

"No way. Okay, so she's a lesbian. She's no killer. Think about it. You ride with her almost every day. You know her."

Jeff looked at his shoes.

"I…I can't refute the evidence." He looked up. "I need time to think." Head slumped downward he walked away leaving Mary alone.

This stinks! If Agnes is a killer I'm Humpty Dumpty! She needed to talk to Agnes. *And I'm not fuckin' cracked.*

†

Cochetta sat in the interview room holding Agnes's rosary in the palm of her hand. The beads looked like they were made of some type of horn, polished to a bright shine. Tiny shamrocks adorned each bead. Cochetta was unfamiliar with the meaning of the beads, but they were obviously important to Agnes, important enough that she carried them with her. Stuffing them into her front pocket, she grabbed the case folder. The earlier adrenaline rush was wearing off, and was quickly being replaced by a headache.

Pushing open the interview room door, the Ranger was immediately bombarded with flashing lights. Several reporters shoved microphones toward her face. She let them clamor for a few minutes before holding up her hands.

"One at a time, please."

A man directly in front of her jammed a long microphone in front of her.

"Is Lt. Kelly-Elliott really the Rapture Killer? Has she officially been charged?"

Cochetta nodded her head.

"Looks like there's a leak in the police department. Yes, Ms. Kelly-Elliott has been charged with three murders. There could be additional charges added once we complete our investigation. Presently she'll be held in county lockup until arraignment. You'll be notified of an official news conference once we have more details. I have nothing else to say right now." Cochetta felt the ache behind her eyes bloom, causing her to squint against the glaring lights. "Any further questions should be submitted to Ranger Lou Chapman at the Texas Rangers Company B headquarters."

Ignoring other questions being shouted at her, Cochetta pushed through the crowd toward the exit at the end of the hall. As she reached for the door it was pulled open from the other side. Jeff Roberts stared at her from the other side.

"That was good work in there, Detective Roberts. I could use someone like you on my task force. You must have a lot of insight into Miss Elliott's personality."

Jeff blinked.

"Her last name is Kelly-Elliott, and I'm not sure—"

"You're a good cop, Roberts. I know this was hard for you. No doubt you're conflicted but you need to do your job."

Jeff looked away for a moment before returning to meet her gaze. His eyes expressed his unspoken pain.

"I'll do my job. Don't expect me to be all gung-ho, though. Agnes is still my friend."

"Understandable. I have no problem with that as long as you stay objective. That's all I ask."

"Fair enough," Jeff said reluctantly. "But if I find out you're wrong about her…"

"I'm not."

"You'd better not be, Ranger Lovejoy. She's not the only one who'll have your ass if I find out you are."

Cochetta's cheek twitched under her right eye.

"I hope you haven't put her on too high a pedestal, detective."

Jeff leaned into Cochetta's personal space.

"You should climb down off yours. Let's get this straight right now. You're arrogant, you're cocky, and you're a bully. I don't like you but I'll work with you to make sure Agnes isn't being railroaded. Something about this doesn't feel right no matter what kind of evidence you have." Jeff turned and stomped away.

Cochetta took a deep breath and tipped her head back to look up into the night sky. A smile tugged at her lips.

I have you, Kelly. It's only a matter of time before you confess.

The Ranger would expose the woman for the monster she was, and the best part was knowing she was right…and, of course, putting an end to the killings.

Chapter 9

Agnes stood with wet hair, in an orange jump suit. White slip-on shoes, one size too big, covered her feet. In her arms were the rest of her county-issued clothing and bedding. She had already been stripped of everything personal. The correction officers had searched inside and out. The humiliation of the body cavity search made her wonder why anyone would commit a crime a second time.

Four Tarrant County guards surrounded her while the warden instructed her on acceptable behavior. Agnes hardly heard a word the man said. Her concern was that she was headed to general population. Cops didn't do well amongst prisoners. Okay, an ex-cop, but that didn't matter. It could still get her killed or at least a good ass kicking. Some of the women prisoners she might have personally arrested. If so, they were going to be very happy to get her on their turf. A hand on her back brought her back to her current surroundings. The big question Agnes had was how the Ranger had arranged all of this. Protective isolation was the normal procedure for any policeperson charged with a crime.

"Pay attention, Elliott," The only female guard in the small room said, nudging Agnes on the arm.

"It's Kelly-Elliott."

"Here it'll be whatever we decide. I suggest you listen to what the warden has to say instead of daydreaming," the guard replied. "His advice can save you a lot of heartburn."

The warden's warning to steer clear of trouble was accurate. His comment about things being all right if she followed the rules wasn't. Prisoners didn't respect rules.

"I'm a cop, Warden. You know what happens to cops in lockup. All the rules in the world won't protect me if I'm put with the general population. I need to be in isolation until my arraignment."

"I agree completely, Ms. Kelly-Elliott. Unfortunately I have orders to the contrary. Until I can clarify them or get the proper authorization to change them we're stuck with what we have. Clearly someone doesn't like you. Just keep a low profile, follow the rules, and you shouldn't have any problems. I'm confident my officers can head off any signs of trouble. Tomorrow I'll make a call or two to see if I can get things changed."

Agnes would've laughed if she had the energy. The warden wasn't going to call anyone. He had full authority to put her anywhere he wanted. Why he was willing to risk her life to accommodate Ranger Lovejoy or whomever she had clout with didn't make sense.

Once the indoctrination speech ended the officers escorted her away. The walk through the quiet halls did nothing to calm her fears. Each jail door that slid open was one step closer to a nightmare. She tried to focus her eyes straight ahead, but her peripheral vision picked up the long rows of cells on both sides after the last door slid shut. Immediately the inmates started their taunting. A few shook the barred cell doors.

"We know who you are, Elliott. News travels fast in here. Everyone's making bets on when you get yours," one woman shouted out.

"She's right," a male guard said. "You're the flavor of the week. Dykes are quite popular in here. You should feel right at home."

A guard behind her laughed.

"Good one, Matt."

Agnes wanted to ask the guards what their problem was when she felt something wet hit the right side of her face and arm. The stench of urine wafted up her nose. Two officers broke off to deal with the assailant. The other two hustled Agnes up two flights of stairs past a gauntlet of verbal abuse and a few flying objects. She was finally pushed into the last cell on the right. The door slid shut behind her. Agnes made the mistake of relaxing.

The body that slammed into her was big, at least a half-foot taller and a lot heavier. Agnes hit the metal bars hard. Her head bounced against a couple and she slid to the floor. Her instinct was to curl into a tight ball to protect her stomach. The roar of inmates' yelling blared as she felt a foot connect painfully…once, then twice.

"Cut it out, Fenton," the guard who had called her dyke yelled. "If she ends up in the hospital ward, you'll be spending time in solitary. Not to mention lose a playmate."

Chapter 10

Cochetta sat entrenched at a makeshift desk in Company B's office. Lou Chapman had placed a piece of plywood over two file cabinets and pilfered a chair from one of the interview rooms for her. Three piles of paperwork and a laptop computer sat in front of her. She had made several solid connections between Agnes Kelly-Elliott's travels and the locations of some victims. A search of the woman's house had produced an elaborate bondage kit. The leather cuffs seemed to match the ligature marks on the victims' wrists and ankles. Thanks to a statewide information campaign, six women had come forward with information about their encounters with the detective.

Cochetta was being hailed by civic leaders as a hero of the people for solving one of the biggest homicide cases in the last several decades.

"Your girl got into some trouble in jail," Lou said as he dropped the *Dallas Morning News* over Cochetta's head onto the desk in front of her. "They've moved her to a private cell."

"What kind of trouble?" she asked, picking up the paper to read where Lou pointed. "Apparently she's okay. A little jail justice might entice her to confess."

"That's a bit cold, isn't it?"

"Tell that to the victims," Cochetta said flatly as she tossed the paper in an ever growing stack next to her chair. The press had been relentless in their pursuit of information about the Rapture Killer. There wasn't a single bit of Agnes's life left in the shadows. Her friends and family had wisely distanced themselves from the situation. Kelly-Elliott was on her own.

"Gonzales called. He wants her moved to solitary. She's still vulnerable to assaults where she's at."

"Has she asked to talk with me yet?"

Lou shook his head.

"No, she's demanding an immediate arraignment hearing. The Police Union refused to represent her. She asked for a public defender. I'm surprised it's taken this long to get one assigned. How did you manage to delay that, let alone prolong the arraignment this long?"

Cochetta shrugged.

"Some judges have a lot of ambition. Add hatred for dirty cops and you can get special, well let's just say dispensation. Elliott's been off the street for almost a week and so far no more bodies have turned up. I'd say that's damn good proof we have the right person. Everyone agrees a confession would make things go a lot smoother. That means a guilty plea."

"You know, Cochise, I've worked with you for only a short time. You're good. Not surprising considering you were put in charge of this case, but I'm not sure I like this side of you." Lou straightened and left without another word.

Cochetta huffed and returned to her work.

"Asshole!" she muttered. Angrily pushing away from the improvised desk she grabbed her hat and coat.

✝

An hour later found her at the Tarrant County Jail. She was informed that prisoner Kelly-Elliott had been taken to the facility infirmary.

"What for? Something else happen to her?"

"Just a follow-up, Ranger. Doc wants to make sure she's recovering from a small incident a couple days ago," the warden explained.

"I read about it in the papers. It didn't sound too serious."

"Oh, that one wasn't. This is another accident. That's why we moved her to a separate cell. She's accident prone." The warden laughed good-naturedly. "She's our prize resident now. Don't want anything serious happening to her, do we?"

Accident-prone my ass! Cochetta thought. "No we don't. It wouldn't look very good on your record."

"Or yours," the warden replied.

"I have nothing to do with this place. You're in charge; you're responsible. As long as her accidents don't raise questions, I don't really care. Now, I'd like to see her. How do I get to the infirmary?"

Cochetta made her way through the halls to the medical wing. Lying on a bed near the entrance was Elliott. A man in a white jacket looked up.

"The warden called ahead, Ranger Lovejoy. She's all yours," he said, moving away.

"Thanks." Turning toward Agnes, Cochetta cocked her head slightly. "You don't look so good, Elliott. You can end all this. Confess and I'll have you transferred to solitary. Perhaps even get the solicitor to agree to life instead of going for the death penalty," Cochetta said, not bothering to waste time with niceties.

Agnes turned her head toward the Ranger.

"You're delusional. There's nothing to confess."

"Listen! You're not a stupid person. In fact, from what I've heard and read, you're pretty smart. We have enough evidence for a conviction. Why delay the inevitable?"

"Fuck off, Lovejoy!"

"That attitude is going to get you more trouble, especially in here," Cochetta barked angrily, pointing her finger at the detective.

Agnes turned her head away.

Cochetta walked up next to the bed and leaned over so she could whisper into Agnes's ear.

"Fine! Play the tough girl. I'm betting there are a lot tougher ladies in here than you. And remember, I can delay your arraignment for several more weeks. Judges don't like crooked cops, especially murderers. When you eventually do get arraigned, your bail will be so high you still won't get out. Personally, I don't think you'll make it another week. You're a coward, and cowards are weak." She then blew softly on Agnes's ear. "A memento for you, **Kelly**...sorry, I mean Agnes. The next time a woman does that, it might not be so nice." Cochetta straightened. "When you're ready to talk, tell the warden. He has my number." Walking away she thought she heard a sob, but dismissed it. Killers didn't deserve consideration.

✝

Agnes listened to the Ranger's fading footsteps.

So the warden's been talking to you. Who else have you enlisted into your little vendetta squad? The last six days had been miserable. She had been in survival mode since the moment she arrived.

The last attack was well organized and particularly brutal. She would never be rid of the scars on her body from the knife wounds. The damage was superficial but deep enough to require a few stitches. At one point during the assault she wished they would just kill her. All her problems would be solved. Unfortunately, self-preservation was the stronger instinct. Fighting for her life she managed to defend herself until the guards showed

49

up. Agnes knew she wasn't safe anywhere in the prison. Even the infirmary had inmates transitioning in and out. Her biggest chance for release would be if the killer struck again, not a prospect Agnes wished on anyone.

†

Agnes was tired…beyond tired. The weeks of incarceration were taking their toll. She didn't know if there was even a word to describe the utter desolation of her situation. Her life consisted of intermittent naps and constant vigilance. She had lost over ten pounds since entering jail. Her initiation into prison life was the beating on the first day. The guards had stopped it, as well as another assault a few days later. She was not so fortunate with the rape. Whether they knew it was happening or not, Agnes wasn't sure. That they ignored it afterward, she was.

†

It happened at the end of the second week of her incarceration. Although she now had her own cell, she was still part of the general population during the day. Normally, she kept a low profile, only taking showers after everyone was finished. Thirty minutes before lockdown meant the other women were taking care of last-minute business, whether it was a final fix for the day or a quick fuck with a girlfriend. Fortunately most of the inmates just wanted to sleep.

Agnes was standing in the shower stall enjoying the warmth of the water beating down on her back. Perhaps that was why she let her guard down. Privacy was a luxury. Eyes closed and facing the wall, she groaned with pleasure as aching muscles relaxed.

"You enjoying yourself, sweetie?" a voice whispered in her ear, startling her. Before she could turn around, she was shoved forward. Her arms were pinned against the wall, her left cheek pressed firmly against the tiles. She didn't recognize the voice but was pretty sure she knew who the assailants were when she saw Karen "Big Tits" Riley smiling lewdly at her. Riley normally hung around with Sylvia "SJ" Jones and Dixie "Dimples" Compton. SJ was the ringleader. She was a large, big-boned woman with scruffy blond hair and a small scar across the left side of her neck, the result of an attack from another woman who had tried to kill her several years before. SJ was a bully, while Big Tits and Dixie acted as her enforcers. Most of the prisoners tried to avoid them. The guards found SJ

50

useful in keeping fights down so they avoided all but the most serious activities she was involved in.

"What do you want, SJ?" Agnes growled, trying to twist her head enough to look at the ringleader.

"Why darlin', you know what I want. Some of that stuff you been hiding." Agnes tensed her muscles trying to lever herself backward but couldn't budge the bodies pressing against her arms and back. "Oh, I love it when a woman struggles. You just keep wiggling that butt of yours like that." SJ rubbed her hands up and down Agnes's back and then moved down to her thighs, first caressing the outside and then the inside. "Oh sweetie, I think you've lost some weight. Not much meat on those bones. Well, I ain't interested in drumsticks. I like pussy. Let's see how tight…"

"Don't!" Agnes yelled, struggling harder. "Don't do this, SJ! This is rape. You'll never get out of here if…"

"If what?" SJ laughed. "Who's going to know? And even if you tell no one's going to believe a perverted, serial killing cop. Or care. Hell, consider yourself lucky I'm your first here. Some aren't as gentle as me."

Before Agnes could respond she felt two fingers shoved inside of her pushing her up onto her toes.

"Oh my, you aren't as tight as I expected," SJ said. "I think she's a three finger, girls." Big Tits and Dimples laughed. "And definitely no virgin." Twisting her fingers she shoved them even deeper. Agnes groaned from the pain of fingernails scraping the sensitive walls and started to scream. A large forearm pressed her head hard against the tiles and a covered her mouth. "Now you don't want to go and attract any more attention, *Detective.* Right now there are only three of us going to fuck you. Make a racket and you might find a few more showing up wanting some pussy, and I know of at least one guard who'd love to put his dick up your ass or anywhere else he wants." To make her point SJ shoved her thumb into Agnes's anus.

"Save some of that for me," Big Tits said. Her voice was normally high but the anticipated excitement made it squeaky.

"I'm next," Dimples said, glaring at Big Tits. "Right, SJ?"

"Sure, Dimps."

"But, I…"

"Shut up, Tits. There's plenty to go around. We have lots of time. JT and Ramsey are distracting the guards. Now, where was I? Oh yeah…" SJ began grinding against the back of Agnes's right butt cheek as she rapidly pumped her fingers in and out. "Oh, baby, this feels so good. I ain't had something like you in a couple of years. If I'd known how good a cop was…"

Agnes didn't know how long the rape lasted, but it felt like an eternity. The other two women had their turns, often complimenting Agnes on whatever part of the body was being groped or assaulted while they laughed and joked with each other. When it was finally over they released her and watched as she slid to the floor, water still pouring from the showerhead.

"Get me that piece of soap over there, Dimps," SJ said. "We need to clean this sweet thing up a bit."

"You going to give her a bath now?" Big Tits asked, sounding surprised.

"Well, it wouldn't be right, or smart, just leaving the blood or her here like this after all of us have been inside of her, now would it? Grab her legs and spread them."

†

No one was around when the guards found her curled up in a fetal position on the floor of the shower.

"You really need to be more careful, Elliott," one of them said sarcastically. "Slipping in the shower can get you hurt, eh Jimmy?" Nudging his partner with his elbow they both laughed and then ordered her to get to her feet. All Agnes could do was lie on the tiled floor and shiver.

"Shit, Karl, she ain't getting up, and I sure as hell don't want to get my uniform wet."

"Get Fenton and Romelly in here. They can drag her back to her cell. And tell Fenton to bring some of Elliott's clothes. We don't want the cameras showing us mistreating a prisoner."

"That's all we need. Another investigation. Damn women think they're somehow entitled to special consideration."

Karl nodded and then grabbed his companion's arm pulling him slightly away from Agnes.

"Listen, Ernie. This is the third attack on Elliott. Put the word out that she's to be left alone for now. The shit's going to hit the fan if someone carries this too far. No privileges to anyone that lays a hand on her."

"Gotcha." Ernie left to get the two inmates.

†

Agnes was unceremoniously dumped onto her bunk. After the guards left, Fenton warned her to keep her mouth shut. She hadn't been part of the rape but she had no reason to stop it either, especially since Agnes was the main reason she was in jail. Her testimony had been crucial to Fenton's conviction.

Not knowing how long she would be locked up, Agnes took the woman's advice. She really didn't have a choice. If she was to survive she was going to have to play by the rules, the inmates' rules.

Chapter 11

Cochetta was having a bad week, one of the worst since she had been assigned to the Rapture Killer cases. First, she had been sure the detective would confess after a few days in lockup. That was almost three weeks ago. She was aware her tactics were a bit unethical; unorthodox she preferred to think, necessary if they kept other women from being killed. Cochetta could live with herself.

Then Captain Gonzales showed up on Thursday demanding Agnes be moved to solitary. He seemed to be the only one openly challenging the evidence Cochetta had accumulated. Having a senior local police officer doubting a Ranger was aggravating, especially when that Ranger was her.

When the warden called, Cochetta anticipated good news.

"Has she confessed?"

"No. She's a pretty stubborn woman but things have settled down a bit. I've ordered the guards to crack down on the other prisoners. Elliott is off limits. She can't keep having accidents."

Cochetta's jaw clenched. *No she can't!*

"Make sure of it," she growled. "I'm getting a bunch of crap from her ex-supervisor. The last thing we want is to move her out of the general population before she tells us what we want to know."

"You'd better be right about her," the warden said. "I'll let you know if things change." Before Cochetta could reply he hung up.

Asshole!

The final straw was a call from a person identifying herself as Agnes's attorney. An arraignment was scheduled in four days. There would be no more delays. The woman was clearly pissed, threatening all sorts of lawsuits because her client hadn't gotten her due process.

"And I want Ms. Kelly-Elliott transferred to solitary immediately, Ranger Lovejoy. If anything else happens to her I'm holding you personally responsible. I've sent a request to the governor demanding a special investigation as to why a police officer was in the prison's general population when such an action puts her at grave risk."

"You'll have to take that up with the war—"

"No, you'll have to," the attorney replied coldly. "You put her in county lockup, now you're going to make sure she receives the protection she's entitled to. Innocent until proven guilty, Ranger, or have you forgotten that?" the attorney asked sarcastically and hung up before Cochetta could reply.

"That's twice someone's hung up on me today," Cochetta grumbled. "I hate lawyers."

†

Cochetta put on her best suit. The black flannel coat with matching vest and pants was contrasted by a stark white shirt and her best white Stetson hat. A thin black and silver bolo completed her look along with her western-style holster hanging low on her hip and tied around her thigh. The silver Ranger badge sat squarely over her left breast.

News cameras flashed and whirred at her as she walked up the courthouse steps. She stopped to answer a couple of questions from local reporters before entering the rotunda. Flashing her ID to the security guard stationed at the entrance she bypassed the metal detector. The courtroom was crowded. Reporters and a few select press photographers huddled in clusters whispering amongst themselves. This was a historic day. One of the nation's most prolific female serial killers was about to be officially charged.

Agnes was escorted into the room between two beefy guards that probably outweighed her by at least a hundred pounds each. A female corrections officer followed behind them. Agnes looked pale and withdrawn. Both wrists were shackled together, and a chain wrapped around her waist held them close to her body. Her ankles were also shackled. A young woman who looked to be barely out of law school stepped forward and conversed quickly with Agnes before the court clerk called the case.

"The State of Texas versus Agnes Mary Kelly-Elliott!" the clerk announced. The room hushed as the defendant and her attorney stepped forward.

"How does the defendant plea?" the judge asked, not looking up from the file in front of him.

"My client pleads not guilty, Your Honor," the woman next to Agnes replied.

The cameras snapped and whirred. The gavel hit wood over and over as the crowd in the room erupted in a muffled clamor. Cochetta recognized several of the victims' family members attending. They were clearly angry with the plea. She didn't blame them. No one wanted a long drawn out trial.

The District Attorney himself was overseeing the case and stood to speak.

"The State requests that the defendant be held without bail, Your Honor. The nature of these crimes is heinous, and Ms. Kelly-Elliott no longer has any connections to the community. We believe she is a strong flight risk."

The judge finally looked up.

"I understand Ms. Kelly-Elliott is a member of a respected law enforcement family in Ft. Worth," he said. "How is it the State considers her a flight risk?"

"Her family has informed me they want nothing to do with the defendant. That eliminates all reasons for her to stay in the area."

"I see."

"I object, Your Honor," Agnes's attorney called out. "What or how the family feels has nothing to do with these proceedings. Ms. Kelly-Elliott is also a respected police officer and part of this community for many years."

"That may be true, Ms. Schultz, but courts have the responsibility to protect the public. Ms. Kelly-Elliott, you are remanded back to county, but to make sure your rights are maintained, bail is set at one million dollars." The judge's gavel gave a final solid bang on the well-worn wood block on the bench.

✝

God damn it! Cochetta thought. *She could be out with a hundred thousand dollar bond if someone's willing to take the chance.* The likelihood of it happening was small but it was still annoying. She watched as Agnes was led away. Cochetta turned and scooted out the back door, almost bumping into a woman leaving at the same time. She excused herself and made her way to the prisoner holding area of the courthouse. Somehow, she had to convince Elliott to change her plea.

Chapter 12

At the back of the courtroom sat the one person who knew Agnes was innocent. When she stood up to leave her shoulder brushed against the well-dressed Ranger standing near the exit.

"Pardon," the Ranger said, flashing an apologetic smile. The woman felt a rush she hadn't experienced in several weeks but simply nodded her head. It wouldn't do to spend too much time with the famous Cochetta Lovejoy, even though it might be tempting.

For weeks she had fought her cravings for the physical pleasures of the body. Really, she had tried. Trinity River was supposed to be her last. After that, she avoided temptation and concentrated on her work. Unfortunately, her job took her to places filled with sinners. Sinners were what God demanded of her. In time, her own unnatural urges would be forgiven, as long as she saved those with the same perversions. They only needed to understand their sins before they died, and, of course, repent.

No one seemed to appreciate the importance of her role in saving souls. The priests urged Marcella to turn herself in to the authorities or seek help from therapists. The church offered to provide counseling. What arrogant blasphemy! If God's own representatives didn't understand her mission, how could sinners?

She was livid the first time a priest suggested she go to the police. Insignificant humans who did nothing to promote God's will. Couldn't they see that He had given her an enormous responsibility and burden? Lesbians were a malignancy, an unnatural horrendous blight on humanity. She was His instrument, His sword of righteousness, and His executioner. Police! The thought was almost laughable.

†

When Agnes was first arrested Marcella felt relief. Finally she was released from her calling. The voice in her head disappeared. God no longer talked to her. Eventually, though, an unbearable loneliness crept in.

57

Why He was punishing her was unfathomable. Then, yesterday, He returned. Overwhelmed with joy, she willingly agreed to find him another soul.

Marcella walked the half block to her car. She checked the immediate area, making sure no one was nearby, before opening the trunk. Under a blanket was a woman, bound and gagged.

"Can't have you freezing to death, can I," Marcella said, tucking the blanket tighter around her captive. "He wouldn't like that. Besides, we're friends now? God sent me to find you. Why else would He have allowed us to meet at Sister's Delight?" The bar had been crowded. The woman looked uncomfortable, out of place. Marcella could tell she wasn't a regular. "You looked so lonely. That's over now. You have me. I'm your friend. I know you don't understand but you will. I just have one more stop to make. Then we can be together," she said, a bit too sweetly. The woman stared groggily at her before drifting back to sleep. The drugs were working well.

Marcella slammed the trunk lid shut, remembering all the times she had done this before. The first two sacrifices had bothered her, at least a little. Those afterward were much easier. She accepted her duty. God's will could not be denied. Obedience made her strong. Saving souls, well, what greater calling was there, even if it meant killing? Besides this was different. Lesbians were born into sin, wired wrong. They couldn't be blamed for what they were, but that wasn't an excuse for what they did. Humans could control their dark obsessions. When they didn't, someone had to help them. God had chosen Marcella to cleanse lesbians of their unnatural behavior. Once they repented she sent their souls onward, forgiven for all their trespasses. In time hers would be forgiven also.

Marcella slipped behind the wheel of her car.

I know you don't understand, she thought. *The others didn't at first but the eventually saw the light. Like them you'll thank me too. Then you'll be with Him.* Marcella glanced at her watch and quickly started the engine. *Business before pleasure, though.*

She needed to wrap up a sale at one of the gyms she regularly marketed to. Selling physical fitness equipment paid the bills and allowed her the freedom to travel around the state. Fortunately, this particular establishment was only a short distance from a park, and this park had lots of trees, which provided seclusion. Few people frequented the area during the cooler months.

Parking in the empty lot, she grabbed her briefcase and walked to the back of the vehicle to check the woman one more time. When she groaned, Marcella opened a small bag lying next to her captive.

"Now-now, we don't want you attracting unwanted attention while I'm away," Marcella said, pulling out a syringe filled with a clear liquid. "Another little nap will make you feel better." Stabbing the needle into her captive's arm she pressed the plunger. "There. I'll be back soon. You won't be alone much longer."

†

Marcella was good at her job, a natural saleswoman. Her enthusiasm and passion for fitness made selling gym equipment easy. She understood the science of the technology and the theories of proper training. The body was a temple of God and should be treated as such. Her basement was filled with state-of-the-art exercise machines. At least three times a week she started her morning with an hour or more of circuit training. Physical strength was necessary to accomplish her spiritual work.

Fifteen minutes after renewing a service contract and obtaining a purchase order for three new gym sets Marcella was back in her car heading out of the park.

"I had a dream the other night," she muttered, absently talking to the woman locked in the trunk. "God spoke to me. He asked me a question. If his son died for our sins, could we do no less? At first, I thought he wanted me to kill myself but then I remembered suicide was a mortal sin. He wants more from me. I must work harder to prove my worth."

Chapter 13

After a short discussion with the correction officers in charge of Agnes, Cochetta was shown to the holding cell.

"You don't look so good," she said.

"Vacations do that," Agnes replied sarcastically. "Maybe you should take one. I'm sure you'd like the accommodations."

Cochetta ignored the comment. She wasn't going to waste time matching wits with a killer.

"Why do you want to put these families through a trial? Why not just confess? The evidence is solid."

Agnes lifted angry eyes and looked directly at Cochetta. "Solid? You don't have any witnesses, any DNA, anything substantial."

"We have enough to put you away for a long time even if we can't get the death penalty."

"My attorney says otherwise."

"Then she's doing you a disservice," Cochetta said.

"No, Ranger, you're doing the disservice. I'm…not…guilty. Your killer is still out there. Maybe she's moved on to somewhere else but she won't stop. Think about that the next time you look down at another dead girl."

Cochetta slammed her palm against the cell's bars.

"You're a stubborn fool, Elliott. You've been locked up for a month. There have been no more killings. That says it all. I can make things easier for you if you cooperate. Play hardball and the only ones who'll suffer are you and those families. Last month will seem like a day in the park! End this now and save yourself from any more problems."

"I don't need to be saved from anything but you, Ranger. I can live with my decisions. Can you?" Agnes turned her back. The conversation was finished.

Furious, Cochetta stormed away.

✝

The Texas Star Motel could be described as modest. It was clean, but small and cramped. Jeff stood just inside the motel room. The manager had called the police, frantic about one of his rooms being vandalized during the night. When the uniformed officers arrived, they found blood everywhere. The coppery scent was unmistakable.

Jeff hated this part of his job. Red stains covered the carpet. Puddles of blood could be seen on the bathroom floor starting inside the door. One officer told him the tub and shower liner were also smeared. Jeff waited for a technician to bring him booties for his shoes. They were essential to keep cross-contamination away from the scene.

The sound of vomiting caught his attention. A responding policeman was outside puking. When he straightened up, he looked away, embarrassed.

"This your first?" The man nodded. "Don't feel bad. We've all done that."

I wish Agnes were here. It was still hard to believe that she was a killer, but the evidence said otherwise. Slipping on the shoe covers he carefully stepped around the room, avoiding as much of the blood as possible. It wasn't easy. Some had already congealed into sloppy, blackish-red pools. Jeff had no doubt this was a murder scene. The problem was there wasn't a body. *No one survives this much blood loss.*

"Is it human?"

The tech nodded. "Oh yeah! Can't say if it's all from one person, though. The lab will let you know ASAP."

"Thanks." Jeff began making notes. "Whoever did this—" When his cell phone rang, he frowned. "Roberts," he answered brusquely, irritated by the interruption. "Oh, hi Captain. Another? Where?…Okay. Tell the Ranger it'll be about twenty minutes." Flipping the phone shut he shook his head.

"Another body," he said to the technician. "It's going to be a long day." Especially with Lovejoy present.

✝

Cochetta was notified at midmorning that another body consistent with the Rapture Killer's MO had turned up. She wasn't happy.

Kneeling, Cochetta couldn't miss the cross carved on the forehead. The eyes were wide open. There was also bruising around the wrists and ankles. This victim, however, showed a major deviation that was extremely troubling. Two large incisions were carved in a T across the torso. The cuts were so deep the internal organs were exposed.

"That took something sharp," she muttered, more to herself than Jeff. "When was she discovered?"

"A little over an hour ago. I have a good idea where she was killed. I just left a motel room that was covered with blood. If this is the Rapture Killer—"

"This body's different," Cochetta cut in. "The Rapture victims died of suffocation, with only minor mutilations. This woman was gutted."

"Well, that's about the only thing that's different. Everything else matches the MO."

"It's a copycat."

"Maybe," Jeff said. "Or…"

"Or?"

"The Rapture Killer is escalating."

Cochetta angrily pushed herself up from the kneeling position.

"You too? First your captain and now you're defending her. Elliott is the Rapture Killer. She probably has an accomplice. I don't understand how you can still doubt the evidence."

Jeff motioned toward the victim.

"This gives me a very good reason for doubt. Another body and Agnes is locked up. The press is going to love this," Jeff said. "Two Rapture Killers."

"You're jumping to conclusions, Detective."

Cochetta let the sheet fall back down to cover the dead woman.

"Well, if she has a partner, why wait so long to do another? It's been over a month since the last. That only makes Agnes look less guilty."

The Ranger began pacing back and forth; an accomplice was the only thing that made sense.

"It could be a copycat killer. Someone looking to make a name for him or her self," She speculated, "but I don't think so. Elliott has a partner. Why the person waited, who knows? Serial killers aren't the most predictable people. Putting doubts on her guilt makes perfect sense. Hell, she even told us this was going to happen."

Jeff shook his head.

"Another possibility is you're wrong. If so, Agnes would know the killer wasn't going to stop." He gave a visible shiver. "That motel room… Whoever did this likes it messy."

Cochetta rubbed her eyes tiredly.

"I hate this shit! Okay, let's go back to the motel. I want to see that crime scene."

Nodding, Jeff motioned toward his vehicle.

"I'll bring you back to pick up your car afterward," he suggested.

"I'll follow you."

Jeff shrugged.

"Have it your way."

✝

"Shit," Cochetta muttered when she walked into the room. "I need the pictures and lab work as soon as possible."

"I'll have copies on your desk as soon as I get them."

"Good. I'm going to see Elliott again. She has to be involved."

"I think you're wrong about her."

"Just get me what I asked for."

"Yes, ma'am." Jeff mock saluted Cochetta and abruptly turned away.

Cochetta shook her head. This murder was going to complicate her case against Elliott, she thought. Still she felt she had enough evidence to win a conviction.

"I've got my killer. This is the accomplice." *I hope!*

Chapter 14

Agnes was unceremoniously pulled from her lunch and pushed into a small interview room. She was firmly shackled to the chair.

Just in case I develop some kind of super power and escape, she thought drolly. Ranger Lovejoy walked into the room a few minutes later.

"Sorry to pull you away from your lunch." Cochetta's smile said otherwise.

I bet! Agnes decided to ignore Lovejoy. She didn't have anything to say to the Ranger.

"No sense of humor, Elliott? Too bad! I hear this is a fun place." Cochetta opened a folder she brought with her and spread several photos on the table. "I want you to tell me about your friend."

Agnes refused to look at the pictures. She knew her prediction had finally come true. Another woman had died but she got no joy in the knowledge.

"Not talking? Well, I haven't been able to match you up with the other victims, yet, but I know why. You have an accomplice. With you out of the picture, he or she is having all the fun on their own." Cochetta tapped one of the photos. "And a bit more creative."

Agnes's eyes fell to the photo under the Ranger's finger. She felt physically ill when she saw the mutilation.

"My God," she whispered.

"Who's doing this? A protégé? Someone who hates women more than you?"

"I had nothing to do with that, and I don't hate women."

"I suppose a female attorney changed that. Do you like her?" Cochetta asked, suddenly changing the topic.

Agnes ignored the taunt. She leaned forward to look at the other pictures.

"The killer's escalating." Agnes glanced up. "How does it feel being responsible for another death?"

"I wouldn't know. You tell me." Cochetta leaned back in her chair.

"I can't. You're responsible for this woman, only you're too stupid to know it. You're wrong, Lovejoy."

Cochetta laughed out loud.

"About you? No, I have all the proof I need."

"Your proof got flushed down the toilet. All I need to do is sit here and wait for the next body to show up. The more there are, the weaker your so-called proof."

"It will stand up to scrutiny. Now that I know about your accomplice I'll catch her or him too. When I do I'll strike a deal to seal your conviction." Cochetta picked up the photos and stuffed them in the folder.

"Why do you hate me so much? Because I scared you? Your proof, as you call it, can be applied to you, too. Where were you when some of these killings occurred? Why were you in Houston the night we met? It wasn't a sightseeing tour."

"I was planning on getting laid," Cochetta replied coldly. "That's not a crime. Then I met you. You're a freak. What happened that night? Did you chicken out or was I your first?"

Agnes rolled her eyes.

"You outweigh me by what, Ranger? Thirty pounds? By your own admission you can take care of yourself. Why feel so threatened? You can't really believe I intended on killing you."

"That's exactly what I think. We both know what happened in that hotel. For a few minutes you had the advantage."

"And if I had been a killer I would have used it." Agnes rolled her shoulders and sat back as far as the manacles would allow her to. "I was there to lay a woman who seemed agreeable at the time. You! Then you got cold feet."

"You tied me up," Cochetta countered, pointing an accusatory finger at Agnes.

"Tied? No, I used wrist restraints, remember? You didn't really object then. Even gave me your safe word. Apache, wasn't it? You called it out rather quickly. I'd even say panicky." Agnes smiled humorlessly. Cochetta stood, knocking her chair back against the door with a loud bang. "What's the matter, Ranger? You don't like hearing the truth? Or maybe you don't like knowing you're an easy target." Agnes looked up at the camera in the corner of the room. "I'm done." It took only a couple of seconds before the door behind her opened and three guards came in. Agnes took one final look at Cochetta before leaving. "Be careful, Ranger. I might not survive this and then you'll have one more body on that list of yours, only this time you might end up on the wrong side of the bars."

Agnes quietly left through the door leaving Cochetta standing alone in the small room.

Chapter 15

Tom Boiz was a seemingly innocuous club set in the center of Arlington, Texas. It was the kind of place you wandered into without thinking, and then discovered you were in the midst of women who preferred the company of other women. Marcella Salvatore abhorred this type of establishment but they served her needs. Five days had gone by since her last offering. He was now demanding another. She hated that she had to hunt closer to home, but had no choice. God chose the time and place, not her.

Her last endeavor had been messy but satisfying. She still felt the excitement of the knife slicing through soft skin. Blood flowed like crimson rivers flooding the landscape of the body bucking beneath her. The ride was exhilarating. Unfortunately, the woman died too quickly. The next one wouldn't be so unlucky.

Marcella watched the club's patrons closely searching for a sign, something to show her who He wanted. She already knew it wasn't going to be anyone with a group. Witnesses could threaten her mission. So would a confident woman. They were fighters.

There you are, she thought, eyeing a petite blonde standing alone at the bar. Her heart quickened. Edging closer she caught a faint scent of perfume.

"You're new here," Marcella heard the bartender say. "I don't recall seeing you before."

Shyly the woman nodded.

"I heard about this place from a friend."

"Well, glad to see you. Always good to see new faces."

When the bartender moved away, Marcella signaled her over and ordered a martini. Then she turned and smiled at the young woman.

"I couldn't help but overhear you're new to Arlington." *Perfect,* Marcella thought as the woman smiled back at her.

✝

Something was eating at Cochetta. The softly droning TV couldn't stop her from thinking about her conversation with Agnes a few days earlier. What the woman had said was uncomfortably closer to the truth than she cared to admit. She had panicked when Agnes strapped the cuffs around her wrists. And she had consented at first, but realized she had made a terrible mistake. Okay, so Agnes quickly removed the restraints when Cochetta said the safe word. What did that prove? Cochetta didn't like self-doubt.

"Fuck!" she said, throwing the TV remote across the room. The evidence pointed to Agnes. She had the opportunity and the motive. Other women had stepped forward who had not only had sex with Agnes but felt their lives were in danger at the time of the encounters. Like Cochetta, they were uncomfortable with bondage. The problem was, like her, Agnes had immediately released them when they said the safe word. The defense would tear them to pieces. As for the detective's closeted lifestyle, it wasn't unusual considering the prevalent prejudices in her occupation. Most gays and lesbians went to great lengths to keep their sexuality a secret.

Hell, I should be her defense attorney, Cochetta thought. *I'm making her case for her. Damn it! I know I have the right person.*

But did she? Another victim had turned up. Every piece of evidence pointed to the Rapture Killer. Even she couldn't ignore that. Still, she wasn't quite willing to admit she was wrong. If, and that was a big if, Agnes wasn't the killer, Cochetta had made a terrible mistake. A sudden news flash on the television interrupted the Ranger's thoughts.

"Good evening. This is an exclusive report brought to you live from News Central." The scene quickly switched to a female reporter standing in front of a sign that said Meadowbrook Golf Course.

"Good evening. This is Mandy Cobern. A woman's body was found a short while ago at the Meadowbrook Golf Club."

Cochetta rushed to the TV to turn up the volume.

"The police aren't giving any details yet, however, several witnesses described the victim's hands as being in a prayer position and a cross carved on the forehead, similar to victims of the Rapture Killer. This is the second body since Detective Kelly-Elliott was charged five weeks ago. Some are now questioning whether the former Ft. Worth police detective is guilty. Did the Texas Ranger really catch the Rapture Killer or is an innocent woman being held because of a horrible blunder. Stay tuned for an exclusive report..."

Grabbing her hat and keys, Cochetta rushed from her motel room. She needed to talk to the Arlington detectives investigating the scene.

✝

Lou Chapman tossed a plain manila envelope on Cochetta's desk, startling her.

"This arrived for you from Arlington PD."

Cochetta rocked back in her chair and picked up the envelope, impressed at how quickly the department had gotten copies of the information to her. Tearing open the flap, she pulled out a neat stack of papers and several photos.

"Thanks."

Lou peered over her shoulder and grimaced as she shuffled through the pictures. Setting them aside, she read the report.

"She has to have an accomplice."

Plucking the report from Cochetta's hand he flipped through it until he reached the coroner's report.

"Maybe, maybe not. You're stubborn, Cochetta, and hardheaded. All of this indicates she's not the killer. Even if you can put her at fifty percent of the crime scenes, you won't be able to explain these to a jury. I suggest we release the detective and move on."

Chapter 16

Sitting in the prison library Agnes deliberately kept her head down as she read the headlines on one of the six newspapers available to the jail population. The less attention she attracted the less she got. For the most part the correctional officers left her alone. The inmates seemed to have lost interest in her and were now focusing on a couple of new arrivals. Fresh meat always attracted predators and Agnes, for now, seemed like three-day-old roadkill, not that she was complaining. Whatever the reason the prisoners had moved on was fine.

The headlines in the papers said two more women had been killed in the Dallas-Ft. Worth area.

I bet Lovejoy's unhappy about that, Agnes thought. *I wonder what her latest theory—*

"Elliott!" a gruff voice called out, startling her.

Agnes jumped and glared at the guard who had just yelled her name. He was dangling a set of manacles from his fingers.

"You have a visitor."

Agnes shook her head.

"I'm not interested in seeing anyone."

A female guard appeared next to the hulking man.

"You don't make the decisions here, Elliott. Get a move on it. I don't want to use this on you." She tapped the Taser in the holster on her hip.

Agnes sighed and stood. She walked to a wall and placed her hands flat against it. The guards shackled her hands to a chain they had placed around her waist and led her from the library. She walked between them in silence, eventually ending up at a room numbered

503. Unlike others in the prison, it didn't have a nameplate on the door.

"Where are we?" she asked, hoping she wasn't being led into some setup for another assault. Things seemed to have settled down but that didn't mean anything, especially since she suspected that one or two of her guards had intentionally conspired with her attackers. Law enforcement didn't like bad cops any more than prisoners.

"We were told to get you. That's all we know," the man replied as he knocked on the door.

Stepping inside Agnes was surprised to see her former captain sitting in a heavy metal chair.

"What now? I've already received my release from duty," she said. "Or did you want to tell me personally that I've been dismissed from the force, Captain?" The man rose and slowly approached her.

Michael Gonzales looked past Agnes to the guards standing slightly behind her.

"Take the chains off and get out."

Both guards looked at the third person in the room for confirmation. When he nodded they did as the police captain had ordered. Agnes looked at the other man seated behind a small steel desk. She recognized him as the jail's assistant administrator. The few times she had met him had been after her beatings, but not the rape. Either he didn't know about it or decided to distance himself from that situation. Agnes swore she would have him fired if she ever got out.

The shackles were removed from her wrists and waist. Agnes stood in her jumpsuit and slip-on sneakers staring first at the administrator and then shifting her gaze to the captain. She refused to give them the satisfaction of speaking first. Captain Gonzales shifted uncomfortably and then sighed.

"What the hell happened to you?" he asked, noticing how thin she was.

"I'm dieting," Agnes said sarcastically. "What do you want? You aren't here because you missed me."

"You're free," he said quietly.

"Free?" Agnes was stunned.

"Yes. As soon as you change into your street clothes you're out of here." Gonzales handed her a plastic bag.

"Just like that?" Agnes pushed the bag away. Things didn't happen that easily. "Is this another one of Lovejoy's games?"

"No. Go change and let's get out of here. I'll explain everything in the car."

"I want to see the release order," Agnes said, refusing to fall prey to one of the Ranger's tricks. She didn't trust anyone now, including her previous supervisor. Captain Gonzales walked over to the desk and yanked a paper out from under the administrator's hands. He held it out to Agnes. She took the paper and reviewed it. "I don't get it."

"You're free to go, Agnes. It's over."

"You caught the killer?"

"Not yet," Gonzales said sadly. "But you're no longer a suspect. All the charges against you have been dropped. You've been cleared."

"Cleared by whom?"

Gonzales's head dropped.

"Lovejoy."

Agnes laughed but not from amusement.

"You're joking!" She looked at the Ranger's crony who was sitting quietly nearby. For some odd reason she felt she could believe him. During his visits to her he had hinted that her cooperation with Lovejoy would be beneficial to her well-being. He would know what the Ranger was up to.

"Is it true?"

The man leaned back in his chair and rocked backward.

"She talked with a judge this morning."

Without another word, Agnes grabbed the bag out of the captain's hand. Five minutes later she was dressed, not caring who saw her in her underwear. Her clothes hung off her like oversized bags. Gathering her jail clothes, she walked angrily over to the administrator and flung them at him.

"You're a fucking asshole and don't think I won't remember our little talks," she said and then turned to Captain Gonzales. "So you're taking me home?"

Gonzales sighed.

"I have to ask you to sign some papers first." He held up a folded document. "The city—"

"Can kiss my ass!" Agnes hissed, grabbing the papers and glancing quickly over the first page. She sank into the chair the police captain had occupied earlier and read the offer. "My pension? They'll give me my pension?" She looked up. "You've got to be kidding me! They think I'm just going to sign this and go away? This wasn't a fucking vacation. It was an unimaginable hell!" She tossed the documents on the floor. "Let me tell you what I want, Captain. My life back! My job! The respect of my fellow officers, my family and friends, and I especially want Lovejoy's ass on a fucking border patrol in the middle of nowhere! Now if you can't do that, at least let me borrow a phone so I can call a goddamned cab."

Gonzales bent down and picked up the documents.

"I'll drive you anywhere you want to go."

Chapter 17

The order to release Elliott didn't make Cochetta happy. She felt like tearing her hair out. The case was stalled. Her main suspect was innocent and the Ranger was no closer to the killer than before. The Ft. Worth Police Department tried to keep Elliott's release out of the press, but failed. No one was directly accused of misconduct. Even the papers knew they needed miserably. The Rapture Killer was big news. Falsely accusing and charging a Ft. Worth police officer was even bigger, especially considering the time she had been locked up. Local newspapers were having a heyday, alluding to the Rangers' and police department's investigative incompetency to walk a fine line if they expected future cooperation. Editorial commentaries, however, were harsher, questioning how such a mistake could happen. Sadly, the papers seemed less interested in Agnes, the person. Her name appeared only a few times, mostly stating that Detective Kelly-Elliott could not be reached for comment or her present status as an officer hadn't been determined yet.

Cochetta fully expected Elliott to come after her. She was almost disappointed when she didn't. A call from Captain Gonzales advised her to leave Elliott alone. Cochetta heeded the warning. Until now her record was impeccable. She intended on minimizing the damage. True, she had pulled a lot of strings to keep Elliott locked up, but no one was going to jeopardize their careers by talking. Besides, the Rapture Killer was still at large. More than ever, Cochetta needed to be the one to find her.

Chapter 18

Jeff drove carefully along a narrow road in the rolling hills on the Oklahoma side of the Red River Valley. It reminded him of the drive to his parents' summer home on Canyon Lake in Texas Hill Country. He had spent many wonderful summers there, swimming and fishing. Eventually his parents sold the cabin, using the cash to bail them out of the debt an overly extravagant lifestyle had caused. Lesson learned they put what was left over in a college fund for Jeff, hoping he would follow in his father's footsteps and become an accountant. He didn't.

Tucked in the visor above his head was a handwritten map directing him to a lakeside cabin. A small blue reflector caught his eye as he rounded a sharp bend. The instructions said to turn left at the landmark. The driveway started out as dirt but soon turned to gravel. Anyone at home would hear a vehicle approaching.

The cabin appeared as he came out of a sharp right turn. Agnes was standing on the porch, a coffee cup in one hand. The other hand rested on her hip. She sipped the drink and waited for him to stop before stepping off the porch.

"Are you accepting visitors?" Jeff asked, giving her his most boyish grin.

"If I said no, would you leave?" Agnes tossed what remained in her cup on the dirt.

"Yes, but not before pleading to use the john. I've been driving for hours." He turned the ignition off but remained behind the wheel.

"You must have gotten lost." Agnes glanced up at the low purple clouds rolling across the darkening sky. "Leave now and you might make it to Paris. One of the motels should have a room." She looked back at her ex-partner. He reminded her of a pouting child. "Oh, for Christ's sake come in and piss." She turned and stomped back up the porch, disappearing through the opened door.

Jeff smiled. Grabbing his small travel bag from the passenger seat, he exited his vehicle and followed.

Agnes walked to the sink, not bothering to see if Jeff had followed. She definitely didn't feel up to company. A distant clap of thunder told her a serious storm was moving through.

Damn! He'd have to stay the night too. The dirt roads were dangerous after a rain. Jeff entered the kitchen and dropped his bag on the floor. She pointed to a door almost directly in front of him.

"Bathroom is through there."

He nodded and helped himself to the facilities. When he reappeared he leaned against the kitchen wall watching her as she contemplated the contents of the fridge.

"Since you're going to be staying you get the couch. There's only one bedroom."

"I know." Agnes looked at him over the fridge's door. "Griff told me."

"Griff doesn't know when to mind his own business." *Asshole!* she thought as she pulled a partially thawed chicken out and slammed it into the sink. She had planned to boil it the next day. "Did you draw the short straw or something?" she asked, leaning against the counter and crossing her arms.

"Not really. His department's short this week so he couldn't get time off. He's worried about you. Said I was better than nothing. I had some time off coming to me. Besides, I wanted to talk to you anyway. Have you been keeping up with the case?"

Agnes shook her head.

"Nope! No TV, no radio. And cell reception is crappy."

"Griff said you probably wouldn't."

Agnes walked over to Jeff and gestured to the couch in the little living room.

"And what else did Griff have to say?" Agnes was getting annoyed.

"He told me to tell you to get off your pity pot."

Agnes blinked.

"He's an ass." She sat down at one end of the long couch. Jeff sat at the other. "And I'm not on my pity pot. I'm trying to get my head wrapped around all of this," she said quietly.

"Sorry..." Jeff blushed.

Agnes waved her hand in the air dismissing his apology.

"It's okay. I just need some time." She settled back onto the couch. "So tell me, what's so important you'd drive all the way up here to talk to me? It certainly wasn't because you wanted to check on me." She wasn't sure she wanted to know but a part of her needed the details...the cop part.

"That's not true. I was also—" The glare Agnes gave him shut him up. "Sorry. I know that's hard to believe. Anyway, our killer's escalating, getting bolder." Jeff walked over to his bag and pulled out a thick file. "I snagged this on my way out this morning." He held up the folder.

Agnes held her hand out.

"That's against department regulations."

Jeff shrugged.

"So who's gonna tell?"

"Definitely not me. I don't owe them anything." Agnes smiled as she hefted the file onto her lap. It had doubled in size since she had last seen it nearly two months ago. "She's been busy."

"Like I said, escalating. The last two victims were gutted. Whoever this killer is, we need to find him or her quick."

"I think FBI profiler is right about it being a woman. It makes sense."

Jeff sat silently as Agnes pored over the material.

"You're right about the escalation." Agnes cringed as she viewed the new pictures.

"We've managed to find the crime scenes on several of the victims. She's no longer a neat freak, but she's damn good at not leaving anything of herself behind or picking places where a lot of people are about." Jeff moved closer to Agnes and flipped the pictures until he came to the bloody motel room. "This is where one was murdered. No one was registered to the room but she took a big risk, anyway. We don't know how she got in. There's plenty of DNA strewn about. Unfortunately it could belong to hundreds of people."

Agnes studied the photos and read the CSI reports.

"What kinds of locks are on the doors?"

"Keyed."

"So she knows how to pick locks or stayed there at some time. Have you checked the employee lists present and past?"

"We're working on it."

"Also check the owners, their friends and families, vendors. You know the routine. There's a reason she picked this place and this room."

"I'll bring that up during the next task meeting."

"You made the task force? I'm impressed," Agnes teased.

"Hey! I have skills."

Jeff's hurt expression didn't fool her. Agnes smiled and looked at the list of names in front of her.

"What about other forensics? This woman has to be leaving something behind or taking something with her—you know, Locard's exchange principle."

"That's the problem. If she is, she's picked places that are contaminated by so many people we wouldn't know who to pick as a suspect. The sites where she dumps the bodies are places hundreds of people have visited or stayed. The lab is still categorizing hair, cigarette butts, condoms, beer cans, and just about everything else you can think of. The bodies have been bathed or rinsed off so well trace is almost nonexistent."

"What about interviews?"

"No one at the scenes saw anything. I'm checking out the lesbian bars. I'm a regular at every club and tavern within a fifty-mile radius. The women must think I'm a pervert or one of those guys who think they're lesbians." Jeff looked at Agnes, clearly trying to judge her reaction. "You know that I don't care, right? About you being one, I mean."

Agnes looked up from the file.

"You could have told me that when you first found out. Then I might have believed you. Or at least known I had one friend."

"I am your friend. I was confused, but it was never about your sexuality. Lovejoy had some pretty strong evidence."

"She had nothing. Everyone wanted to catch this killer so badly they were willing to throw anyone under the bus. I happened to be convenient."

"I didn't think—"

"You thought too much. Associating with a suspected lesbian serial killer wouldn't be good for your career?" Agnes said angrily. Jeff looked duly admonished. "Never mind. We haven't known each other that long. I understand putting career first."

"It wasn't about you being a lesbian," Jeff said. "I…well, never mind. Griff seems cool about it, about you I mean."

"Oh, I'm sure he is. He can blame our failed marriage on me now, instead of him cheating with his daughter's fifth-grade teacher." Agnes rose and walked to the kitchen sink where she poked the chicken. "I'm going to start this. It won't be fancy."

"I don't need fancy. I'm just grateful I don't have to go hungry," Jeff said. When his stomach growled loudly, he blushed.

Agnes smiled and then burst out laughing.

"Dinner will be served in about two hours. Hopefully you'll last that long."

Chapter 19

Marcella Salvatore worked her body against the woman beneath her. Rivulets of sweat ran down her cheeks. She was close, so very close to coming. The woman whimpered against the gag in her mouth. Marcella glared angrily at her captive. The noise was distracting.

"Be quiet or I'll never finish." She smiled when the whimpers ceased. "That's better. I can't do this when I'm angry. He wouldn't like that." Marcella once again started to grind against a bruised thigh. As her orgasm built the self-loathing set in. Then the hatred and disgust for the woman she was lying atop of. "This is your fault. You are an abomination to God. If people like you didn't exist, I wouldn't have to do this."

Marcella's movements grew frenzied. Soon, very soon she would be sending God another soul. He would forgive her for her weaknesses, especially those of the flesh.

The first tingle of her pending release began to build. She pressed harder against the slender thigh. When the climax came she tensed, shuddered and finally collapsed onto her victim. The devil surely had a hold on her in the moments like this. She always wanted more. Each time she prayed to God asking him to quell her unnatural desires, and He did for a while but for a price: the soul of the sinner that tempted her.

Marcella pushed angrily up and away from the pitiful body beneath her.

"I don't want to do this, you know? You shouldn't have worn those tight jeans and T-shirt. God says it's wrong for a woman to want another woman but you came looking for one. You wanted to be noticed. To be picked up. Be grateful it was me. I'm saving your soul. He wants me to but only after you feel the pain of sin. Only then can you receive his blessing." Marcella had to be her strongest at this moment. A moment of indecision or doubt could jeopardize all her hard work. She had already secured the woman's belongings in a plastic bag, which was lying on the tiled bathroom floor. Six plastic jugs of water sat next to it; inconvenient, but the abandoned motel had no running water. The woman's ID was tucked away in Marcella's travel bag as a keepsake.

Marcella checked the fillet knife to make sure it was sharp, not that she had any doubts. She had honed her skills until she could put razor edges on any knife. Sports tape was wrapped around the handle providing a secure surface for gripping.

"This is going to hurt. God wasn't happy with the others. They died too quickly. Not enough penance. Not enough pain. At first I didn't understand why He stopped talking to me. Then I realized someone else got the credit for my work. I thought God made a mistake. How foolish of me. He never makes mistakes." She smiled as she again straddled the woman, this time settling her naked body across her victim's hips. "I promised I'd try harder." She ran the thin blade of the knife down the woman's cheek. A thin line of blood chased after the silver tip. The bright red stream trickling from the cut was satisfying. The woman thrashed back and forth, her body twisting.

"Stop that! I'm trying to help you." Marcella made another cut, pushing the blade deeper and then drawing it in the opposite direction of the first slash. Her victim's muffled scream was irritating. "Be quiet! Otherwise, I'll have to do something that really hurts." That irrational expectation was an indication of the degree of Marcella's insanity. No one being carved up could stay still or quiet. The more the woman struggled, the more agitated Marcella grew. Frustrated she slashed crosses on each breast, both thighs and the forehead. Blood poured from the wounds. "Now we're getting somewhere," Marcella said happily, especially knowing she was only getting started…and that the woman was still alive.

†

Lovejoy was bent over vomiting her dinner at the base of a well-groomed crepe myrtle. Jeff stood behind her, facing away, giving her a moment to gather herself into something resembling the seasoned investigator he knew she was. He was only marginally holding his own churning stomach in check. Jeff doused a bunch of paper towels with water from one of the many bottles he kept in his car trunk just for these situations. He also had disinfectant gel, bleach, dish detergent, and several other items. Crime scenes were filthy places.

"Are you all right?" he asked, handing her the towels.

Cochetta nodded and wiped her face.

"Can I have some of that?" she asked, pointing to the bottle in his hand.

"It's all yours."

After rinsing her mouth a few times, she finally took a big swig to soothe the burning in the back of her throat. She capped the bottle and offered it back to the detective.

"Keep it," Jeff said.

"Thanks." Cochetta tucked the bottle under her left arm as she walked back up the gently sloped hill supporting a cell phone tower. The body was lying on the east slope. The flesh had been meticulously sliced down to the bone. Skin and muscle hung like loose grotesque ribbons from every part of the body. "What kind of animal does something like this?"

Jeff couldn't look at the body for more than a second or two. He hoped the photographs would lessen the horror of the image.

"Not an animal. A monster! Your profiler said it was a closeted psychopathic lesbian with religious issues. I'd say she had more than religious ones. And this might not have happened if you hadn't been so goddamned focused on Agnes."

Cochetta stiffened, her eyes flaring.

"The evidence pointed to her. You believed she was guilty just like I did."

"But I wasn't the one who kept her locked up when the next body turned up. Now we have more. Agnes would have been able to add her insight and expertise on this case."

"Speaking of Elliott, I hear you misplaced your field file, Detective," she said, keeping her voice low and even. "You wouldn't want to make a guess where you left it, would you?"

Jeff blinked a few times then shook his head.

"I really can't recall, Ranger Lovejoy."

"I just bet you can't." Cochetta turned and walked to her truck where she dropped the tailgate. Jeff followed several feet behind. She rummaged in the back of the Bronco until she found a well-used map. Unfolding it, she flattened it out and looked at Jeff. "Point!"

Jeff took a deep breath and peered at the map for a moment then looked back up at the Ranger. "I don't understand."

Cochetta crooked her finger at him. When he leaned in closer she grabbed his gray silk tie and pulled.

"Where is she?"

"Who?" Jeff croaked.

"Elliott."

"That's none of your business," he replied, yanking his tie from her hand. "Besides why do you want to know?"

"That's none of **your** business. I'll ask you one more time, and this time as the head of the team that your department assigned you to."

"Since her whereabouts has nothing to do with this case I'm not obligated to tell you anything, Lovejoy. I may be under your command but I still work for Captain Gonzales, and he said you were to stay away from her."

"Well, he isn't here now is he? If you don't want me to have someone else assigned in your place, you'll tell me what I want to know. I'll deal with your captain later."

Jeff hesitated. Lovejoy may not be liked by the Ft. Worth police, but she had a lot of connections that could create problems for him. He glanced down at the map and nervously licked his lips.

"She doesn't want to be bothered," he said reluctantly.

"I don't give a rat's ass what she wants. I need to talk to her. You're the quickest way to find her. What's it going to be, Roberts? Her location or your position on the investigation!"

Slowly he extended his finger and pointed to a small lake on the other side of the Red River.

Cochetta grabbed the map and pushed Jeff backward away from her. She slammed shut the tailgate.

"Smart decision. Write down the directions. I'll be back in a couple of days."

Jeff worked his fingers under his much too tight tie.

"She's not going to like this. What if we find another body?"

"Take notes! Take pictures! Do your job!" Cochetta climbed into her truck and started the engine. "You're the one who said she could give us a different perspective. I'm going to see if you're right."

Left standing by himself, Jeff felt he had again betrayed Agnes.

Chapter 20

Griff heard the crunch of the gravel under tires well before the dirty white Bronco made its turn toward the cabin. He had received a frantic phone call from Jeff Roberts explaining what had happened. Giving his own supervisor an ultimatum of approving personal leave or him calling in sick anyway, his captain reluctantly approved the time off. After throwing a few pieces of clothing in a backpack Griff sped off to warn Agnes.

The old chair was comfortable. He rocked slowly back and forth, smoking his favorite pipe, which was stuffed with sweet tobacco. Griff hadn't had the pleasure of meeting the famous Ranger Lovejoy and was looking forward to this opportunity. As she climbed out of her SUV he took his time evaluating her. Light blue crystalline eyes regarded him with equal interest and suspicion. He met her gaze openly. There wasn't much that could unhinge Griffin Elliott.

"Can I help you, miss?" He offered good-naturedly with a smile and a puff of his pipe. The woman came right up the porch steps and casually leaned against the rail in front of him. She was one of the tallest women he had ever seen, and extraordinarily attractive. *Few things more beautiful than a deadly snake,* he thought.

"I'm looking for someone but I might be lost."

"Well, I'd say you found someone. Lost I can't say." He extended his hand. "Griff Elliott." His hand hung steadily in the space between them, waiting patiently to be taken in a friendly shake.

"Elliott?" The Ranger asked as she slowly extended her own hand.

"Yup." Griff nodded. Her firm grip met with his approval. "And I bet you're Ranger Lovejoy. I've heard a lot about you." He smiled at the look of annoyance that momentarily crossed her face.

Surprised you, eh? he thought, feeling smug. God he loved to be one up on someone, especially a holier-than-thou Texas Ranger. She released his hand and crossed her arms. A forced smile etched her lips.

"I'm sorry that I can't say the same of you."

"Sucks doesn't it?" Griff said, standing. "Let's go inside and get out of this chill." He set his pipe down in a stone ashtray before turning away from the Ranger.

Cochetta remained leaning against the porch rail for a few minutes after the man entered the cabin. The door remained open in invitation. She hated being at the disadvantage. Pushing away from the rail, she cautiously stepped inside. A quick scan of the sparse but functional interior left her a bit confused. Griff wasn't anywhere to be found.

"He went out back."

Cochetta spun to her left where she found a very weary-looking Agnes pointing a very intimidating shotgun at her.

"Put your gun over there," Agnes instructed, motioning with the barrel of the shotgun at the small wooden table just to Cochetta's right.

"I don't think so."

A neat click and the press of something solid at the back of her head caused her to hold her breath.

"I think so," Griff said as he gave the Ranger's head a little prod with the barrel of his service revolver. "Go easy, Ranger. The little woman over there is a bit edgy. I suggest you just do as she says." Cochetta held her left hand up and away from her body as she carefully used her right hand to unsnap the strap of her holster. Easing it out, she purposefully kept her fingers clear of the trigger. "That a girl. Now that wasn't so hard," he said when she placed it gently on a cloth mat. "Put your left hand on top of your head, and your right hand behind your back."

"Like hell I will!" Cochetta barely got the words out of her mouth when she found herself efficiently turned into the wall beside the open door. Her right wrist was cuffed before she had come to a stop, and her left arm was twisted sharply backward. The remaining cuff snapped over her wrist locking her hands behind her.

"Don't fuck with me, Ranger," he instructed. "I'm not like Roberts or those other wimps you're used to pushing around. I push back, only harder. Now go over there and sit on the couch." Griff uncocked his gun and winked at Agnes. "I thought you said she was tough."

Agnes shrugged.

"I said she had a reputation for being tough."

"Like most, a bit overblown. I'd say she's not that smart either, letting herself get captured so easily," he scoffed. "If this gets out it would take her down a few pegs." He looked down on the seated Ranger who was brooding. "I'm going back outside. Aggie doesn't allow smoking in here, but if I hear one thing that remotely sounds like a threat, I'll be back, and I won't be happy. Do we understand one another, Ranger Lovejoy?"

"Perfectly," Cochetta growled.

Griff looked at Agnes.

"Apparently she does have some sense. You good?"

"I'm okay. Thanks." Agnes smiled gratefully at him.

"Call me if you need me." He gave one final warning glance at the Ranger, and left.

✝

Agnes took a deep breath. Slowly exhaling she set the shotgun against the wall next to her chair.

"He doesn't trust me," she said. Agnes nodded toward the shotgun. "He has the shells. I guess he thought I might lose it if you pissed me off. What do you want, Lovejoy?"

Cochetta looked like she was about to pout.

"Who is that guy?"

"My ex." Agnes leaned forward, resting her elbows on her knees. "Not that it's any of your business. Now, answer my question."

"I'm looking for Roberts' missing file."

"And what makes you think it's here?"

"Is it?" Cochetta asked.

Agnes pulled open a small drawer on the end table beside her. Pulling out the file she tossed it onto the coffee table.

"Anything else? It's a long drive for something you already have copies of."

"Insight."

"I'm not a cop anymore, remember?"

"You've been cleared. It won't be long before you're back solving crimes," Cochetta replied, somewhat sarcastically.

"Are you really that stupid?" Agnes asked. "The city doesn't think it wise to take me back. Or should I say I'd be an embarrassment. A constant reminder of their incompetence. By the way, thanks for the firsthand experience of our justice system from the other side. Maybe you'll get a chance to try it out," Agnes said angrily. "I can only hope. As far as insight, kiss my ass."

"I was doing my job," Cochetta replied defensively. "You would have done the same thing."

"No. I would have done a lot more investigation before coming to a conclusion. And I definitely wouldn't have pulled any strings to make the accused's life a living hell because of some personal vendetta. You played the system to exact revenge on me. You're a coward." Agnes stood and began to pace back and forth as her agitation grew. Cochetta had to crane her neck to keep track of Agnes as she walked the length of the cabin and back. Agnes stopped, her eyes closed as she tried to calm herself. "Now I want you to leave me alone."

"There's a killer out there. A killer who's just like you!" Cochetta had no idea where Agnes got the strength but she was soon on the end of a solid punch that landed across her left cheek, glancing off her nose. "What the fuck!"

Agnes stood, shaking her right hand as Griff barged into the cabin from the porch. He pointed sharply at Agnes.

"Are you fuckin' nuts? Sit your scrawny ass down," he ordered, pointing to a chair. Turning to Cochetta, he examined her face and nose. Blood spilled over her lips and down her chin onto her starched white shirt. She winced when he touched it. "It's broken."

"Son of a bitch!" Cochetta said, shaking her head, sending bloody spittle all over the front of Griff's shirt.

"Take it easy. I'll set it for you. Let me get some ice and a rag to clean you up." He looked over to where Agnes sat looking blankly at her swelling hand. "Aggie, you okay?"

Agnes looked up at him with watery eyes and nodded.

"Go ahead, help her. I'm going for a walk." She rose from the chair and walked out the front door.

Griff watched her leave and then turned back to look at the Ranger who was still bleeding. "Come on, lean forward, I'll get those cuffs off you."

"They weren't necessary. I wasn't here to hurt her," Cochetta said, turning her head and wiping her chin on her shoulder. A smear of red was left behind.

"I hope not. You've done enough of that already. I wasn't going to take any chances. She's not in a good place, Lovejoy. You ruined her life in a way she'll never recover from." Griff unlocked his cuffs from Cochetta's wrists and placed them in his back pocket.

Cochetta remained silent as he walked to the kitchen sink. She had to find a way to get some insight into this killer. Agnes was her best bet, or so she thought. Now she wasn't sure. The woman was obviously unstable.

"I'm a real piece of work, huh?"

Griff shrugged.

"You could've handled things better. I don't understand how you can head up an investigative team and be this stupid. It's almost like all of this was personal." He cleaned up the Ranger's face and then handed her a soft cloth. "This is going to hurt a lot, but better to set it now than later. He quickly grabbed Cochetta's nose along the bridge and aligned it.

"JESUS!" Cochetta gasped, knocking his hand away.

"Life's a bitch, ain't it?" Griff leaned in to look at his work. "That should do it. As good as new. Now don't touch it until I get back with some tape."

†

Agnes sat on a fallen tree near the lapping water of the lake. Her hand throbbed. She couldn't believe she had been provoked into violence so easily, but had to admit it felt good.

"Hey, slugger." Griff's gravelly voice came from behind her. "How's the hand?"

"Hurts," Agnes said, shrugging. "Is she okay?"

Griff sat on the log next to her and gently took her injured hand in his and checked for broken bones.

"She'll live. Wiggle your fingers for me."

Agnes gritted her teeth and performed the task stiffly, but without too much pain.

"I think you'll live also," he announced, placing a bag of frozen peas over the knuckles. "Is fighting a lesbian thing?" He asked as he dropped his rear off the log onto the ground, resting his back against the fallen tree.

"It's a pissed off thing, asshole, and don't tell me you wouldn't have done the same thing if you were in my place."

"Probably worse! But this isn't about me, is it?"

"No. I'm not handling this very well am I?"

Griff pressed his lips together in thought.

"Better than I would've done. Listen, Aggie, you should find someone to talk to about all of this. I've heard stories about being in the pen. I'm not asking for any details, but if half of what they say is true you should definitely get a professional to work you through this. Maybe poke around in your head a little."

Agnes stared at her ex in surprise.

"Who the hell are you? And what have you done with the real Griff Elliot?"

Griff grinned.

"I deserve that. I'm working on my own issues. Twice a week, with a psych doctor named Karen and that's all the info you'll get from me about her or my problems."

Agnes couldn't help but smile.

"If I were straight I might consider dating you again."

"Speaking of that…" Griff turned his head to clearly see Agnes, "… was it me? Something I did wrong?"

"You think you turned me gay?" Agnes asked and laughed. "You really think you can change genetics? This Karen is really going to earn her pay."

Griff frowned.

"Well, when you put it like that." He received a gentle slap to the back of his head. "Damn woman! You're gay and violent!"

Agnes shook her head and looked out over the rippling water. The sun was setting, painting the sky in brilliant reds and oranges that flooded the lake with color.

"What should I do about all this, Griff?"

"She wants to know what makes you tick, Aggie. She's wants to catch this killer, and realizes she's wasted a lot of time. For some reason she thinks getting into your mind will give her insight into the killer's."

"And that's supposed to make me feel good?"

"No. What she did must be weighing heavily on her. It would on me, and I'm an asshole."

"So I'm supposed to just cowgirl up and help her? Like nothing ever happened? I can't do that. What she put me through…" Agnes couldn't finish the sentence and shook her head. "I *won't*."

Griff shrugged his broad shoulders and looked at the lake.

"You're smart, Aggie. Real smart. You might be able to save another woman's life. You think outside of the box and, well, you do have insight into how a lesbian and a religious person might think."

"That's not fair," Agnes grumbled, looking back over her shoulder at the cabin. "Damn it!" She rose from the log cradling her injured hand against the bag of thawing peas. "Give me about twenty minutes with her. I promise I won't hit her again. But I'm not going to be nice."

Griff tilted his head back to look at her.

"That's my girl."

"Go to hell." Agnes dismissed him and trudged up to the cabin.

"Love you too, darlin'!" Griff smiled to himself and then looked back at the lake.

Chapter 21

Cochetta sat on the sofa holding her aching head in her hands.

Where had everything gone so wrong? At least three more women had lost their lives because of her blind hatred for Elliott.

Why? Because she made me uncomfortable? She warned me. I still agreed and then freaked out. I've destroyed her life and God knows how many others. "I'm a real piece of work," she muttered.

"They say admitting it is the beginning of getting over it."

Cochetta's head swung in the direction of the open front door.

"I don't know what to say."

Agnes blinked and softly closed the door.

"There's nothing you can say. It'll just piss me off more. I promised Griff I wouldn't hit you again so it's best you keep this conversation professional." Agnes moved to crouch in front of the fireplace and put two small logs on the burning embers; a few pokes and the fire began to grow, pushing warmth into the quickly cooling cabin. She sat in her chair, the peas still wrapped around her hand. "You have ten minutes. I'll answer what I can if I think it's relevant…and don't fuck with me. I'm pretty sure I could get off on an insanity plea this time." Her expression told Cochetta that she was serious.

"Do you know why she's doing this?"

"I can guess. She probably thinks she's sending God damaged souls. She arranges the bodies so they can witness Christ's arrival. According to scripture he's supposed to come from the east. The dead will rise first." Agnes had given herself a refresher course in religious studies while in jail. "Their eyes are pinned open so they can see His Second Coming…or watch the killer doing her dirty work. My guess is the latter. The dead's eyes don't need to be open to see Christ."

"Do you think she's Catholic, like you?" Cochetta picked up Jeff's folder and then fumbled in her shirt pocket for a pen. The top was smeared with blood. She wiped it off on her jeans and then clicked the top.

"How the hell am I supposed to know that? She's obviously Christian, but what denomination is anybody's guess. If she's a practicing Catholic and this fanatical, she's confessing to someone. She must travel a lot, either for her job or she's well off."

Cochetta thought about that for a moment.

"Where would she go to confess?"

Agnes rubbed her eyes with her left hand.

"A priest or a minister. They're obligated to keep quiet. Pretty much any denomination is. I'd make a list of churches and cathedrals around the area. Also, see if there's a locational pattern to the killings. Time, too. This woman, if it is a woman, is smart. And don't waste your time trying to intimidate the priests or clergy. They would encourage her to turn herself in."

Cochetta nodded as she took notes. When she finished she looked up, making eye contact with Agnes.

"Why did you…you know…tie…restrain me?" Cochetta asked softly.

"We've covered that," Agnes answered shortly.

"I need to understand things. Why is control so important to you?"

"You're kidding me, right? That's what you're all about. If your conscience is bothering you go get analyzed by someone else."

Cochetta stiffened.

"I'm fine with my conscience. I want to know why people are into bondage. Then maybe I can figure out this killer."

"Bondage is about the control, Ranger, but by both participants. That's why there's a safe word. I set the pace and choose the location. It satisfies my needs. In a way I own the person for a little while, and they own me. Two sinners on equal terms so to speak."

"But the Rapture Killer takes it further."

"Yeah, for some reason something went horribly wrong with her. Either she was abused or someone taught her this behavior. Kill the sinner and the sin goes away. Absolution, for a while. Then the craving returns, only stronger."

Cochetta felt sick.

"What about the new twist in the killing? The extreme mutilations."

Agnes leaned back in her chair.

"I don't know. Maybe she likes what she's doing now. There's no explaining crazy."

Cochetta sat silently thinking for a while. The killer wasn't the only thing bothering her.

"Do you need anything? If I—"

Agnes looked directly at Cochetta.

"You can fuckin' resign," Agnes replied coldly. "I think we're finished here. You'd better leave before it gets too dark. These back roads can be tricky at night."

Cochetta grabbed Jeff's file and tucked her pen back in the bloody shirt pocket. The front door swung open. Griff walked in accompanied by a gust of winter wind.

"All done, Aggie?" he asked, clearing the doorway, but holding it open. Cochetta stood and retrieved her gun from the table. When Agnes didn't answer, he looked at the Ranger. "I guess you'd better be on your way."

"I'm leaving." Cochetta took one last look at Agnes who had curled up into the chair and was staring at the flickering fire. She looked back at Griff.

"If I can do anything…" Cochetta trailed off.

"Just catch the killer, and leave her alone. She has to work this out for herself." Griff motioned for her to follow him outside. "Listen, Ranger, you screwed up royally and Aggie paid a terrible price. You're lucky she even talked to you. I would have killed you if you'd done that to me, but then again I'm not Aggie."

Giving her a nod he went back inside the cabin and shut the door, clearly an indication that she should leave.

Chapter 22

Marcella wasn't happy.

If it hadn't been for that damn flat, she thought, and instantly regretted the cursing. God didn't like swearing.

Her trip to Odessa had started well. Three gyms wanted to replace their outdated treadmills and ellipticals. Also, the sports director at the university was interested in setting up a small private exercise room for the staff. She managed to complete her business quicker than she had anticipated. Her commissions from the sales would cover several months of expenses. All in all it had been a great two days.

The first night in town, however, was the real icing on the cake. God was making it easier and easier to pick up women. One more night of pleasure…one more sinner saved. Could it get any better?

†

She first saw the motel on her way to Odessa. The windows were boarded up. Always on the lookout for potential sites to complete her missions, Marcella stopped to check it out. The doors to several rooms were unlocked. Inside each was an overwhelming musty odor. Furniture covered with thick layers of undisturbed dust was evidence that no one had been around for a long time. One room still had an old mattress covered by a filthy stained sheet. That was easily remedied.

Perfect! Satisfied, Marcella returned to her vehicle and continued on. Somewhere in Odessa a young woman was waiting to be saved.

†

Dragging the unconscious woman into the room was exhausting. Normally Marcella picked more petite victims. They were easier to move. After yanking the sheet off the bed, she strapped the arms and legs to the different corners. Standing back she stared at the spread-eagled body and smiled.

You'll thank me for this.

Lighting several candles, she placed them around the room. The eerie glow was satisfying. The stage was now set for her to begin.

Ritual was important to Marcella. She removed her clothes, folded each garment neatly before placing them in a plastic bag along with her boots. Her travel kit sat on an old broken nightstand. Once naked she sat down on the edge of the bed and waited. When the restrained woman started twitching, Marcella reached over to pat the pudgy cheek.

"Wake up," she ordered. "I can't do this if you aren't awake. You have to know why you're here." Marcella stroked her own pubic area and shivered. The skin was velvety soft, completely free of hair. God had told her she had to be clean. At her hotel she had depilated her head and body. Afterward, she scrubbed every inch of skin.

Mounting the semiconscious woman she rubbed her breasts against the body beneath her. The excitement grew, and with it guilt, the guilt of pleasure. A low moan escaped between her victim's lips.

Whore! Marcella thought angrily. Leaning back she stared hard at the woman's face. *All that makeup. It's disgusting.*

"Shut up! Or I'll shut you up," she said when she heard a groan. "Pleasure is my reward, not yours." She reached into her travel bag and pulled out a long thin knife. "Listen, I haven't hurt you, yet," Marcella said, changing her tactic. "You enjoy sex? Of course you do. You just moaned." Testing the blade with her thumb, she smiled her satisfaction at the sharp edge and then laughed. If this were a movie, it would show her cutting herself, but that was ridiculous. Why would she mutilate her thumb? Only an idiot wouldn't recognize a sharp knife. Another moan distracted her from her mental meandering.

"If you keep that up I'll have to do something awful. You don't want that do you?" she asked, pressing the knife's edge against the woman's throat. Drawing it lightly over the skin she felt a sense of exhilaration when blood oozed from the small wound. The woman jerked her head sideways trying to twist onto her side. Infuriated, Marcella drove the blade deep into her captive's throat, severing the cartilage and vocal chords. "Now, see what you've done! See what you've done!" Marcella screamed. Yanking the knife out she felt the body buck a few times before sagging back onto the bed. Staring at the blood pouring from the wound Marcella shuddered. God wouldn't be happy.

Too quick. I know I've failed you but it wasn't my fault. She wouldn't listen. Please forgive me, Marcella pleaded. When she heard no voice, Marcella smiled. *Thank you. Oh, thank you. I knew you'd be pleased with her. All that makeup. And those piercings. It was disgusting.*

Besides, hadn't she satisfied her own physical needs? If He wasn't happy she wouldn't have had an orgasm. Remembering the intense moment she felt another coming on. God knew how to reward her. Did He have sexual urges, she wondered. Immediately regretting the thought, she felt a sense of panic.

"I'm sorry," she cried out, looking upward toward the ceiling. "Please forgive me." Looking back at the body Marcella felt the rage building again. "You made me think that! You want to corrupt me like you've corrupted others." Raising the knife she hacked at the soft flesh wanting to see the rich red blood flow. If God wanted blood, then blood he would have. It would be messy but she had planned for that. She always planned out everything. Mistakes were unacceptable.

†

On the second day, with her business finalized, Marcella decided to head home. It was late evening. Marcella was used to driving the long roads across Texas. A person could drive for hours without seeing another vehicle, especially at night. There were few cops on the deserted highways so she didn't have to worry about getting a speeding ticket. If she drove most of the night she'd be able to turn in Hector's car and get hers out of the shop. It had been there for over a week.

She smiled thinking of Hector. One day she'd probably marry the man, not that she loved him. He was rich, though. With offices all over the state, he had a fleet of vehicles at his disposal…and hers when she needed one. Money didn't buy happiness but you sure could afford your misery.

When the Eurythmics' song "Sweet Dreams" began playing on the radio, she sang along. "Some of them want to use you, some of them want to get used by you…"

The words took her back to the abandoned motel room she had spent several glorious hours in.

Night had settled in by the time Marcella saw the lights of the truck stop. Her gas gauge registered slightly over a quarter of a tank. Dallas was still a good six hours away. Yawning, she regretted her decision to drive back home this evening. Another night in the hotel wouldn't have hurt anything.

Pulling next to the pump, she climbed out and stretched. Once the tank was filled Marcella wandered into the restaurant searching for the bathroom. Then she bought a couple bottles of water.

"You want a bag for those?" the cashier asked.

"No thanks." Marcella grabbed the bottles. She pushed open the door and stepped into the cool night air. A sliver of moon was barely peeking over the horizon.

Maybe I should just stop at the next motel, she thought, not looking forward to another six hours on the road. It was going to be a long, boring ride.

"Excuse me, miss." Startled, Marcella jumped and swung around. "Sorry, I didn't mean to scare you," a young woman said.

She was wearing an old, oversized denim jacket with matching blue jeans. A knit cap was pulled down covering the top of her ears. One hand was tucked in her pocket. The other clutched a rolled up newspaper. She looked barely older than twenty. "Are you heading toward Dallas?"

"I might be," Marcella said cautiously. "Why?"

The girl looked down for a few seconds and then back up to Marcella's eyes.

"I was wondering if I could catch a ride. I don't have much money but I can pay you something."

"Sorry, I don't pick up hitchhikers," Marcella said. "Besides, you shouldn't be asking strangers for lifts."

"I don't normally. This is actually the first time. Guess I'm not too good at it, huh?"

"Guess you aren't, so why are you?"

"My boyfriend was visiting his mom, and was in an accident. I'm trying to get to the hospital to see him."

"Oh, is it serious?"

"No, well a little bit. He broke his hip. He'll be there awhile."

Love, Marcella thought. *One day I'll meet someone. God wants us to love.*

"You care that much about him that you're willing to put yourself in danger?" When the girl gave her a sheepish smile, Marcella relented. "Oh, all right! It'll be good to have company." She motioned toward her car. "Let's go. My name's Marcella, what's yours?"

"Madeline."

"Madeline. Well, Madeline, you said this is the first time you've hitchhiked?" Marcella asked once the girl had settled into the passenger seat.

"Yeah."

"So why choose me? There were other people at that stop. I'm sure some were heading toward Dallas."

"You looked nice and you're a woman."

"And you think women can't be dangerous?"

"Oh, I'm not that naïve. My friends gave me some good tips on how to protect myself."

"Like what?"

"Well, first I was told to avoid men if possible, except maybe really old ones. And don't get in the front seat if there's someone in the back unless maybe it's an old woman."

"Sounds a bit complicated," Marcella said, giving her passenger a curious glance. "So old people are safe."

"Yeah. Most women, too! At least statistically women aren't as likely to be murderers and definitely not rapists."

"True but it only takes one, you know."

"I know but I have a secret weapon." Madeline proudly held up her rolled newspaper.

"A newspaper? You going to beat someone to death with that?"

Madeline laughed and pulled something out of her pocket.

"No, but if I set it on fire in the car, the driver has to stop, doesn't he?"

Surprised, Marcella nodded. It actually was a great concept.

"I'm impressed! I hope you don't plan on lighting that thing in here," she teased.

Shoving the lighter back in her pocket, Madeline grinned.

"Naw…not unless you're a killer or something."

"Not to worry," Marcella said. "You're perfectly safe with me. Why not lean back and nap a bit. We've a long way to go."

Taking her advice, Madeline leaned the seat back and closed her eyes. Within minutes she was asleep. Marcella looked in the rearview mirror before turning to glance at her traveling companion. Smiling, she began humming to herself.

†

About forty minutes into the drive, Marcella heard a muted pop and felt the car swerve to the right. Gripping the steering wheel, she pressed steadily on the brakes making sure not to lock them up. As the car slowed she guided it off the pavement onto the shoulder.

"What happened?" Madeline asked, shifting her seat upright.

"I think we just got a flat tire." Marcella reached into the glove compartment and pulled out a flashlight. "Let's go look." Walking around to the passenger side she met Madeline by the front wheel. "Know how to change a tire?" she asked, kicking at the tire.

"Not really. Do you?"

"I've done a few. I need to get a few things from the trunk. Stay here and hold the flashlight." Minutes later she returned carrying a screw jack, lug wrench and rolling the spare. "This goes under here," she said, positioning the jack under the car. And the wrench goes here." Turning the wrench the tire cleared the ground. "That's the easy part. Now all I need to do is loosen the lug nuts, slip the tire off, and put on the spare." Marcella quickly demonstrated the procedure. "Would you put this in the trunk while I tighten the nuts," she asked, pointing to the damaged tire.

"Sure," Madeline said, handing Marcella the flashlight. Rolling the tire toward the back she leaned it against bumper and she peered into the open trunk. Two wool blankets were neatly folded on the left side. Not wanting to get them dirty, Madeline picked them up and laid them over the fender. Then she grabbed what looked like a tool bag by one handle and started to drag it toward her. When it tipped over the contents spilled onto the floor.

"Oh gosh!" she exclaimed, embarrassed. Then she stared at the items. Duct tape, syringes and vials filled with a yellow liquid lay next to a roll of twine, two fillet knives, a handheld knife sharpener, and surgical gloves. Glancing around the trunk interior, she saw a roll of clear plastic next to a box of trash bags. Frightened, Madeline straightened up. "Why…why would you—"

"I'm sorry you had to see that," Marcella's voice said from behind her. Madeline never had a chance to respond. A sharp blow across her shoulders sent her flying forward almost landing in the trunk. Twisting, her body slid sideways onto the ground.

✝

Seconds after she sent Madeline for the tire Marcella knew she had made a mistake. Easing the lug wrench from the jack she stood and tiptoed toward the rear of the car. When she saw Madeline straighten, she knew she had no choice. Swinging the lug wrench at the girl's head, the blow missed, hitting her across the shoulders. Madeline collapsed onto the ground.

"I shouldn't have been so careless," Marcella said, chastising herself. She had never killed anyone without God's permission. Madeline wasn't a sinner, at least not like the others. "What do I do now?" She stared nervously at the woman lying at her feet. Kneeling she probed along the neck searching for a pulse. "I can't just leave you here and I can't take you with me." Looking around she searched for a place to hide the body. The mesquite trees would provide some cover but unless she could bury the body vultures would attract any passerby's attention. Without a shovel, it would be impossible to dig a grave. There was no way to cover up tire tracks, footprints or any other evidence. She had no choice but to take Madeline with her.

Grabbing the duct tape, she bound the girl's wrists and ankles. Then she gathered up the spilled items and threw them into the bag. After hefting the flat tire into the tire well, she replaced the trunk floorboard and tossed the blankets back in. Just as she bent to lift Madeline, Marcella saw lights coming toward her. Unable to judge the distance in the dark she wasn't sure how far away the vehicle was. It could be several miles but at seventy to eighty mph, it would reach her in minutes. Even if she had time to get Madeline into the trunk the passing vehicle might stop to see if she needed help. That was the last thing Madeline wanted to deal with. She wasn't about to risk possible identification by someone later, especially if they had seen the girl getting into her car at the gas station. Her only choice now was to leave Madeline behind.

✝

Nothing is quite as dark as the open roads at night across the vast scrublands of west Texas. Grayson Jones was on his way back to his ranch after an evening of cards and drinking with his friends in Midland-Odessa. It wasn't often he went to the city, but the recent rains had brought a lot of things to a halt on his small spread. The trip provided some much-needed companionship. His ancient CB

104

radio chirped at him from his dash while one of the more powerful AM stations broadcasted classic country music. Occasionally he would sing along to keep his eyes open and his mind on the road.

The clouds had cleared, leaving a canopy of stars. Gray silently berated himself for not taking his friend's offer to spend the night. He glanced down at his odometer and then back at the road, noticing what looked like disappearing red taillights in the distance. Minutes later he saw a large object lying next to the road. At first he thought it was a dead deer but quickly realized it wasn't. Slamming on his brakes, he skidded to a halt.

"Damn!" he swore, jumping from the vehicle. The body of a young woman was lying on the shoulder only a few feet from the pavement. Gray was sure she must have been hit by a car, possibly the one he just glimpsed. *Hit and run? What would someone be doing out here this time of the night?* Stooping, he groaned as his knees crackled. "Miss! Miss!" he said gently, rolling her on her side. It was then he saw the duct tape around her wrists. "What the hell!" When she moaned and opened her eyes, he saw fear and then relief. Gray unwrapped her wrists. Whatever had happened, it was a matter for the police. In the meantime, he needed to get her to the hospital in Odessa.

Chapter 23

Cochetta sat up in bed, awakened from a drug-induced sleep by the ringing of her cell phone. She had recently started taking sleeping pills. It was the only way to stop thinking for a few hours.

"What?" she growled.

"Cochetta? This is George."

"What's up?"

"Dispatch just got a call from the Odessa Sheriff's Department. A young woman was found several miles outside the city limits. She's at the hospital. The doctor said she was hysterical, ranting about a woman with a carving knife and duct tape. I know it's a long shot but I have a gut feeling she may have just run into our killer."

"You want me to go to Odessa? Now?" Cochetta asked, surprised and slightly irritated.

"Might as well, unless you've come up with any better leads. I've arranged for one of our planes to take you. A Corporal Dori Lambert will pick you up at the other end."

"Crap! When do I have to be at the airport?"

"Forty minutes."

Cochetta snapped her flip phone shut and cursed. The combination of exhaustion and the sleeping pill made her feel groggy. A slight headache wasn't helping.

†

The flight to Odessa was a little bumpy but uneventful. Cpl. Lambert was waiting outside the hanger. On the way to the hospital she filled Cochetta in on what the police knew so far.

"Do you think this could be the Rapture Killer?" Dori asked.

"I have no idea. Let's see what the victim has to say."

"Here we are," the corporal said, pulling into the hospital parking lot. "She's in the emergency wing."

Once inside the Ranger sent Lambert to get an update from the two officers leaning against the nurses' station. Cochetta headed toward Emergency to check on the victim. A police officer was standing near the privacy curtain glancing through a magazine.

"She in there?"

"Last time I checked," the deputy said.

Cochetta frowned but didn't say anything as she brushed aside the thin cloth barrier that hid the bed, a very empty bed. She was about to turn back to the hall when she heard a whimper. Cochetta leaned over the mattress, looking for the source. A small form huddled against the wall.

Madeline Owens was petite. Her riotous curly red hair hung down, nearly concealing frightened blue-green eyes. The hospital nightgown was way too large making her seem even smaller.

"Hi, I'm Ranger Lovejoy," Cochetta said, keeping her voice low and even. Pulling her badge from her belt, she held it up. "I'm here to help you, Madeline." When she crouched down the girl cowered away. "Are you in pain? Do you need the doctor or nurse?" she asked softly.

Cradling her right arm Madeline edged along the wall and huddled next to a cart.

"I want to go home," she whimpered.

"Don't you think you should stay here for a while?" Cochetta tried her best smile. The girl just shook her head back and forth.

"She'll find me here." Madeline pointed to the door.

"No she won't. I have several officers outside. We can protect you here. If you go home we won't be able to. Can you tell me what she looked like?" Cochetta sat on the floor and crossed her legs at the ankles. Madeline sniffled, chewing nervously on her lower lip. "I promise you no one's going to hurt you. Help us get this woman so she can't hurt anyone else." Cochetta fell silent. Madeline had to make her own decision. Minutes passed.

"Will you help us?" Cochetta asked.

"Are you sure she won't come back?"

"Ranger's honor." When Cochetta crossed her heart, Madeline smiled shyly.

"Okay."

"Good! Is your arm hurt?"

"My shoulder," Madeline said. "She hit me in the back with something. The doctor said nothing was broken."

"Did they give you something for pain?"

"Uh-huh."

"Well, let's get you back to bed. We can talk about this later." Cochetta helped the girl to her feet and back onto the gurney. "Get some rest."

†

"Her hair is darker, more brownish." The young woman spoke in a quiet whisper to the forensics artist sitting in front of a laptop. "And her eyes are closer together." When the adjustment was made Madeline gasped. "That's her! That's her, Ranger Lovejoy."

Cochetta stood up from her chair and stretched. Forty-five minutes wasn't a long time to do a composite but it felt that way. She leaned over the girl's shoulder to look at the screen.

"What do you think, Watson?" the Ranger asked the forensic artist, immediately thinking about Sherlock Holmes.

"Caucasian, late twenties, early thirties. Brown hair, tanned skin. It's a decent image. Someone might recognize her." She selected the print button and waited for the sketch to clear the portable printer she had brought with her.

Cochetta gave Madeline's shoulder a pat.

"Great job! Anything else you can remember?"

"Well, she didn't have eyebrows. They were drawn on. You know, like the little old ladies do?"

"I know what you mean." Cochetta gave the girl one last pat on her back. "Go back to bed and get some rest."

Madeline smiled at the Ranger before easing herself up from the chair next to her hospital bed. Climbing on top she pulled the covers up around herself.

"Are you going to catch her?"

"We'll catch her," Cochetta promised. "Do you remember Cpl. Lambert, the nice officer who was with me last night?" Madeline nodded. "She's going to stay here with you for a while."

"Can I call you?" Madeline asked, yawning.

"Sure. Anytime."

"Okay," Madeline said sleepily.

Cochetta motioned for Watson to join her once she finished gathering up her equipment.

"Can you get that out to all the agencies quickly?" she asked once they left the room.

"Done! They'll have it as soon as I get back to my office." Watson hefted her computer bag strap onto her shoulder.

"Thanks for flying up so quickly," Cochetta said. Watson was one of the best artists the Rangers had. The air outside had turned unseasonably warm. "I have to fly back to Ft. Worth today. Detective Roberts and I are canvassing the local clubs and bars. Can you expedite him a copy at the Ft. Worth PD? It may jar a few memories."

"It'll be there by the time you arrive. Why do you think she's hit that area so hard?"

Cochetta shook her head.

"She either lives there or works there. Right now we don't have much. This girl's our best bet. I'm not going to let her down like I did the others."

"Go get her, Cochetta. I can't think of a better person to handle this investigation."

"Thanks." *Better person, huh?* Agnes came to mind and she thought about what the detective had said. *Resign. I can't do that. I made a mistake but I am good at what I do,* she thought as she gazed up at the night sky. *When I get this killer you'll see that. Maybe then you'll understand.*

Chapter 24

Agnes looked at the tall glass doors in front of her. She had reluctantly agreed to a mediation hearing between her and the city. They wanted to make an offer for her incarceration and the resulting injuries. The meeting was at the police department, the last place Agnes wanted to be. Well, next to the last. She knew the city attorneys wanted the psychological advantage.

They'll have to count on something else, she thought, yanking open the precinct door. Stepping inside she bumped into Jeff Roberts.

"Agnes?"

"Hi, Jeff. Sorry. I was a bit preoccupied," Agnes said, giving him a faint smile. He was still an ass but she needed to move on.

"Wow, I thought you were going to stay at that lake forever!" Jeff wrapped his arms around her in a gentle bear hug. When she tensed he immediately let go and stepped back. "Sorry."

Agnes chewed the inside of her cheek.

"No, I'm the one who's sorry. I need time to put all of this behind me but I'm working on it." *Twice a week, with a psychologist named Ron*, she thought to herself. "You on your way out?"

"Yeah, I have a long list of interviews today. I think we're getting closer, Agnes." Jeff took a deep breath, "Look, Lovejoy made a mistake." When Agnes's eyes flared, he held up both hands. "Poor timing. I need to get going. How long are you going to be in town? Maybe we can meet up later."

"Today and tomorrow at least. Then I'm heading back to the cabin."

"Okay, how about dinner tonight. I can catch you up on things."

"That would be a department violation. Besides, like I said, I need time." Although curious, she wasn't sure she was ready to socialize with her ex-partner. The door opened behind them. Agnes smiled at the young woman who entered.

"Hey, Agnes. One of my clients is being harassed by the defendant's insurance company rep. I hate being late but I hate bullies even more."

Agnes held up a hand.

"I just got here myself." She looked at Jeff. "Jeff, this is my lawyer, Cindy Schultz." She waited as the two exchanged a few pleasantries before continuing. "We have to get going. I'll think about this evening, okay?"

"Yeah, sure," Jeff said. "Just…umm, call me, please. Nice to meet you, Ms. Schultz." He tipped his head and left.

"Nice guy," Cindy said. "Single?"

"Yes, and an ass," Agnes replied and immediately felt bad. "Not really. He's the detective working with Lovejoy."

Cindy lost her smile.

"Your ex-partner? Oh well." She shrugged. "Nobody's perfect. Ready?"

"As much as I'm going to be." Agnes took a deep breath.

"I'll see where we're supposed to go." Cindy walked over to the desk sergeant. "Interview two," she announced, returning to stand by Agnes.

"Fuck!"

Cindy's eyebrows shot up.

"Something I should know?"

"That's the room they held me in for over eight hours," Agnes said. Her eyes began to tear up. "I don't think I can—"

Cindy laid a calming hand on her arm.

"Not a problem. I'll tell them to move it to the conference room. I'll do the talking. They'll be nice at first. If that doesn't work, they'll try to provoke you. Don't let them get under your skin. You listen. I'll do the talking."

†

Agnes sat stiffly in a straight back leather chair in a conference room. Next to her was Cindy. Across from them on the opposite side of the table were six dour-faced men, all dressed in expensive business suits, the City of Ft. Worth's attorneys. At the head of the table was the mediator, Mr. Frank Cromwell, an ex-judge and retired lawyer. A court recorder sat off to the side, laptop resting on his lap.

Cindy sat relaxed in her chair looking unphased by the last two hours of discussion. When everything escalated to the point where one city attorney stomped out of the room, she smiled politely but said nothing.

"We all need a break," Cromwell said as he rose from his seat. "Be back here in thirty minutes."

Cindy closed her portfolio and laughed.

"I love a good conniption fit!"

Agnes blinked.

"Do you really think this is fun?" she whispered, leaning close to Cindy's right ear.

"For you? No. For me? Hell yes!" Cindy whispered back. Turning, she smiled at the five remaining men pushing away from the table, "You boys better get your game together."

"It's arbitration, Shultz, not a trial," the lead attorney spat out as he angrily slammed his briefcase shut.

Cindy rocked back in her chair.

"Not yet. I just want y'all to get a good taste of what's to come if we go that far." She stood and scribbled something on a piece of paper, folded it and slid it across the table. "Here's something for you to discuss with your colleagues while you're huddled in the men's room."

The man picked up the folded paper and shoved it into his jacket pocket.

Agnes watched them leave.

"What did you write on that paper?"

"A number." Cindy stacked her belongings,

"What kind of number?" Agnes rose from the chair and grimaced. She wasn't accustomed to sitting still for so long.

"A **big** number. One that will make both of us happy. And if they want to play chicken with me, I have an ace up my sleeve that will have the powers-that-be pissing themselves. Go on back to the hotel, Agnes. There's no reason for you to be here. Nothing's going to be settled today. These boys are pure ego. They'll talk over my offer and come back indignant with blustering threats."

"I don't know how you do this," Agnes said.

"Oh, you get used to arrogant assholes in this job. Go on. Get some rest."

"Thanks."

"My pleasure. Listen, Agnes. Trust me. I'm going to chew them up and spit them out, but only after we play their little game. Besides, if I mess this up, Griff will be writing me tickets every other day."

Agnes left without looking back. She didn't doubt Cindy's expertise. That didn't stop the nausea churning away in her stomach.

Damn you, Lovejoy!

Chapter 25

Griff had just turned around in the elevator of Agnes's hotel when a familiar face smiled at him.

"Hey! Jeff!" He eagerly presented his hand to the young detective. "You going up to see Aggie?"

Jeff returned Griff's sturdy handshake.

"Yeah, I saw her at the precinct earlier." The elevator doors closed. Griff pressed Agnes's floor number. "When I got back she was gone. I heard the city's trying to screw her again."

Griff scowled and nodded.

"Aggie called. I swear I've had just about enough of this shit. They owe her for putting her through hell. That woman dedicated her life to this fuckin' city and they want to sweep this mess under the rug."

"I'm thinking about quitting," Jeff said solemnly.

Griff looked over at Jeff.

"Don't do that. There's no reason for the department to lose two good detectives. I suggest you brush up on your asshole skills, though. You might need them one day." The elevator dinged and the doors slid opened.

Jeff looked dejected as he stepped outside.

"I'm ashamed, Griff. I believed them even though I *knew* better. And Lovejoy is a bigger ass than the mayor. I can barely get through the day knowing what she did to Agnes—"

Griff pulled Jeff to a stop.

"You to listen to me. This isn't about you so get over yourself. Aggie doesn't blame you for what happened. That doesn't mean she isn't pissed at you for doubting her. We let her down. Now we suck up our pride and make things right. Lovejoy is the one who started all of this. She has her own demons to face when this is all over with. Probably even an inquiry board. I can't talk for Agnes, but I'd feel better if you stayed on that task force. Keep an eye on the Ranger and update us on everything else." Griff gave a reaffirming poke of his finger to Jeff's chest. "Now get rid of that sourpuss expression. Agnes doesn't need pity pusses around her." Griff winked and pulled Jeff along with him down the hall toward Agnes's room.

Chapter 26

Jeff walked up to the bar at the Fruit Jar. He was becoming a regular since starting this investigation. The Jar, as it was commonly called, was a gay club that catered to both men and women. One of the bartenders, the owner, was a stocky woman with short-cropped hair and multiple facial piercings.

"Hi Telly," Jeff said. "How're you doing?"

"Couldn't be better, Detective Roberts. Business is good and the tips haven't been too bad so far. Your usual?"

"Yeah." He placed his leather portfolio on the bar and opened it.

"How's the hunt going?" Telly asked, placing a Coke on the counter.

"I have a drawing to show you." Jeff pulled out the facial composite. "Have you seen anyone that looks like her?"

Telly studied the image. Then she walked to the kitchen door and called out. "Hey, Brat! Come here!" She walked back to Jeff. "Brat knows everyone in this neighborhood."

Jeff smiled at the thin girl with wild blond locks. He liked the way she sauntered out of the kitchen and came bounding up beside Telly. As if on cue, the bar door opened and Ranger Lovejoy strolled in.

"You got the message," he called out. "Telly, this is Ranger Lovejoy. She's heading up the investigation. This is Telly and Brat. Telly owns this place."

Cochetta nodded, but didn't speak since the two women had returned to looking at the composite picture.

"I don't think she comes here," Brat said. Jeff's shoulders sagged. Another disappointing day with no leads coming from the composite was discouraging. "She reminds me of a woman I saw at the gym on Stanford though. You know the one?" Brat looked directly at Cochetta.

"The one just south of the tracks?" Cochetta had been in that particular gym a few times while in Ft. Worth. It was women only and open 24/7.

"Yeah, I've seen you there a couple of times." Brat blushed, turning her pale skin a glowing shade of pink.

"I guess I'll have to keep an eye out for you, huh?" Cochetta replied teasingly. Another blush spread across Brat's cheeks. "You say she reminds you…" Her heart raced in her chest. This could be the break they needed.

"Yeah, sort of, but I'm not sure. The lady I'm thinking of has light blond hair and it's shorter. We get a lot of women who look alike. At least to me. I'm not very good with faces."

"Tell me about the one you're thinking about."

"Oh, she's okay, kind of quiet. A little weird looking. She maintains the equipment. She definitely likes to look at the women. No crime against that." Brat shrugged indifferently. "I thought I saw her at Tom Boiz once but, like I said, I'm not sure. You know how bars are…dark. What did she do?"

Jeff and Cochetta exchanged glances.

"Probably nothing," Jeff said, cutting Cochetta off. The last thing Ft. Worth PD needed was a case of mistaken identity by accusing the person of being the Rapture Killer.

"Oh, okay. I wish I could tell you more." She looked directly at Cochetta. "If I think of anything I can let you know."

Cochetta recognized the hint. Pulling out her business card she handed it to Brat.

"Call anytime. The department will get in touch with me. You've been a lot of help. Would you mind giving me your full name and contact information?"

Brat smiled brightly and nodded enthusiastically.

"Oh, sure! I'd be glad to give you my number."

Jeff suppressed a smile. He didn't know much about Lovejoy, and didn't care, but he suspected Brat was quite interested in the Ranger.

Outside of the bar, Cochetta swung around angrily.

"'Probably nothing?' Why didn't you warn her and Telly?"

"And say what?" Jeff asked. "Brat said she looks like a lot of women. The last thing we need is another false arrest lawsuit. Maybe you don't care if the public thinks we're incompetent, but I sure as hell do."

"She has to be the one!" Cochetta insisted.

"Like Agnes was?" Jeff asked. "This time we play it by the book."

Chapter 27

Marcella always wore the conservative black wig that had been styled in a tight bun, much like her mother's when she went to confession. When she arrived, there was a long line of people waiting to have their sins absolved. Marcella took extra care to give them the space and privacy they needed to make things right with God. She remembered her own feeble attempts at penance. Then one day God had answered her. She was to be His servant, His chosen and a savior to those women who lusted after other women. If they could not be saved through their church, they would be saved by Marcella. She was humbled by His confidence in her.

Sitting in an empty pew, she waited patiently for the line to disappear. Her list of minor sins this week wasn't that long. The mortal ones were done to accomplish God's work so she was confident she would be forgiven. How else could she do his work?

The line slowly dwindled until it was just Marcella remaining.

"Thank you, God," she said, taking her place in front of the confessional. Smoothing the front of her black dress she took a deep breath. Inside, one of Christ's representatives was waiting. She opened the door and stepped into the small wooden room. As Marcella knelt she looked about the interior of the dim closet. Confessionals always reminded her of a coffin.

The small screen in front of her lightened as the priest slid back a solid partition. She could barely make out the man's profile in the diffused light.

"Forgive me, Father, for I have sinned. It has been six days since my last confession. I accuse myself of the following sins." Marcella first listed the minor infractions. The priest seemed to give minimal counsel on them, almost as if he didn't want to be bothered with having to listen to her. Her next confession definitely caught his attention. She saw the silhouette of his head jerk upward and then turn toward the screen separating them. Marcella felt a sense of relief and importance. If she had his attention she had God's attention. "I've killed, Father. Twice since my last confession. I still have unnatural urges, sexual urges toward women. I know it's wrong but I can't help myself. Please ask Jesus to forgive me." The silence from the other side of the screen didn't surprise her. "Father?" She heard the priest clearing his throat.

"You say you are sorry for these sins, child, yet you repeat the behavior," he said.

"God demands a sacrifice for my sins so I send Him those sinners He chooses."

"How does he demand this of you, my child?"

"He talks to me in my dreams. And sometimes whispers in my ears. Tells me what I must do."

"And what does God tell you to do?"

"Oh, everything, Father. He tells me…" Marcella described in detail what she had done to her last two victims. "You must absolve me of my sins." The silence that followed was unbearable. Afraid she wouldn't receive absolution she slapped the thin screen with both her hands. "You must!"

"I think you should confess your crimes to the proper authorities," the priest finally said.

"I do not answer to a mortal judgment!" Marcella hissed. "Only God can judge me! I demand absolution, Father."

"I…I absolve you of your sins in the name of the Father, the Son, and the Holy Spirit. Go in peace. Get help, child. Talk to the police." The partition slid shut with a deafening finality.

"My penance! You forgot my penance!" Marcella shouted as she banged on the screen again. Nothing happened. She whispered over and over, willing the partition to slide open. Finally, relenting, she stood. Her knees ached. Stepping out of the confessional she noticed that the church was empty. Normally soothed by the quiet serenity, she now felt agitated. Without receiving penance Marcella didn't know what she was going to do. Her sins would follow her into the afterlife. She sank onto a pew and sat staring at the statue of the crucified Christ on the cross. "I need a sign. Something to show me He's pleased."

Chapter 28

Agnes fidgeted in the overstuffed chair across from Ron Lewis, her psychologist.

"Tell me about Ranger Lovejoy."

"No." Agnes sank further into the cocoon of the chair.

"She is a real sticking point, isn't she?" the doctor asked, making a note in his pad.

"She's an asshole."

Ron let a little smile play along his lips. "I gather as much."

"She's arrogant, self-centered, and a bad cop." Agnes thought about that last observation for a moment. "Okay, I'm not sure about the bad cop part as a whole, but she botched her investigation."

"How?" Ron asked, uncrossing his legs and sitting forward in his chair.

"You're not stupid, Doctor. I wouldn't have been locked up or sitting here if it weren't for her."

"True…to both statements, but you need to own your thoughts. The only way to do that is to say them aloud. Hearing words often puts them in perspective."

"I have a great perspective of Cochetta Lovejoy. She was so focused on me in the beginning that she couldn't see the truth if it slapped her in the head."

"What truth?"

Agnes hesitated. She had already told him about her sexuality but hadn't said anything about Lovejoy's.

"I don't want to talk about it."

"Agnes, the only way to work out issues is to talk about them. Why do you think Ranger Lovejoy was focused on you? Did you two know each other from somewhere else?"

"We…we met…once."

"I see. In your capacity as police officers or under more personal circumstances?"

"Personal."

Ron quietly waited for Agnes to elaborate.

"In a bar. We met in a bar several months before. One thing led to another and—"

"And you had sex."

"No! I mean…we didn't have sex. We were going to but she freaked out." Agnes shook her head. "Okay, let me start from the beginning." Over the next fifteen minutes she explained what had happened. When she finished she waited nervously for his reaction.

"So when she saw you with this victim she panicked a second time. That seems a little extreme for a seasoned law-enforcement officer."

"A little? I'd say a lot!"

"Actually I'd say so, too. I'd like to know more about Ranger Lovejoy. She clearly has some issues that need to be resolved, but this really isn't about her. It's about you moving forward." Ron shifted in his chair. "Listen, Agnes, there's nothing I can say that can change what happened to you. I can't make you feel better. Only you can do that but it's going to take time. Ranger Lovejoy isn't your enemy now. Only you are. Hopefully she'll solve her own problems."

"I don't give a fuck about her problems," Agnes shouted.

"Good! That simplifies things. Let's get back to you. You said she was a bad cop and then seemed to question it. Why?"

"Well, she wouldn't have been assigned to the investigation if she wasn't good."

"And?"

"And yet the minute she saw me she assumed I was guilty. She went out of her way to prove it. Okay, so some of the facts fit but a good officer wouldn't have revealed her hand so quickly, nor jumped to such a fast conclusion. And a *good* officer would have at least made sure I was in isolation while I was locked up. Somehow she was able to manipulate the system so I was put in the general population. Then pulled a few strings to make sure I stayed there longer than necessary. I...I..." Agnes put her head in her hands and trembled. "How am I to forget everything that happened to me?"

"You can't, Agnes. Nothing will wipe those memories away. That doesn't mean they have to control your life. Things will get better."

Agnes shook her head.

"I don't see how."

Ron reached over and patted her hand.

"Trust me on this one. I'm good at what I do. How are your kids doing?"

The sudden change of topics temporarily confused Agnes.

"My children? I...I received a letter from Jenny two weeks ago. She's not coming home for spring break." Agnes looked past the doctor and out the window. "She doesn't want to see me."

"She said that?"

"No. My mother did." Agnes could feel the emotions boil up inside her. "She won't see me either. At least not until I am treated for my *condition*. Mom mailed me a list of facilities that specialize in curing queers. She's always had a strong hold on my kids. I'm not surprised by their behavior."

"Your mother raised you also. You overcame her prejudices."

Agnes frowned.

"I hate being this way." She looked up at Ron. "If I believed for a moment I could be cured of these feelings, I'd sign myself in to one of those places."

"So Ranger Lovejoy outed you. I get a feeling being outed was almost as bad as everything that happened in jail."

Agnes bit her bottom lip.

"It was worse. I can always move away from here. And you're probably right about things getting better with time, but no matter where I go I'll still be a lesbian. My family will have nothing to do with me and I've lost my career. Lovejoy destroyed my life. If I wanted to come out to my family I'd have fucking done it years ago!" Agnes ended with a firm fist pounding on the chair's arm. "Sins repeated knowingly are not absolved." Agnes quietly repeated that statement, "Sins repeated knowingly are not absolved."

"You think your sexuality is a sin?"

"The Bible says it is," Agnes pointed out.

"The Bible was written by men, Agnes, not God."

"But He inspired them," Agnes countered defensively.

Ron shrugged. "That's one opinion."

"For a Christian, it's the one that counts."

Ron tapped his pen against his notebook.

"Have you been to church lately?"

"No."

Ron looked at his watch.

"Maybe you should. It's the only place you'll get absolution…" Dr. Lewis hesitated. "But if you truly believe in a divine being, and in His or Her goodness, remember that the Bible was written a few hundred years ago by a bunch of misogynous, misguided men. You need to make peace with yourself, Agnes. You're the only one that can do that." Glancing at the clock on the wall, Ron slapped his hands on his knees. "Well, I think you've had enough therapy for one day. Please give what we've talked about some thought."

"I will. Thanks, Dr. Lewis. I do feel better."

"Good! Now I have one more suggestion. Eventually you're going to have to decide what you want to do with yourself. If I'm right, it's going to be a lot sooner than later. One more thing. Try not to focus so much on Ranger Lovejoy. She's not your enemy now. You are."

✝

Agnes walked along the lakeshore in quiet contemplation. Cindy, her attorney, had just left. She had driven all afternoon to personally deliver the bad news. The city attorneys were calling her bluff. They wanted a trial.

Enraged, Agnes threw several plates against the wall.

"You said we had a strong case!"

"We do. That doesn't mean they won't do everything they can to scare you. That's their job. Intimidation tactics are an attorney's best tool. Find the weakest link and break it."

"Meaning me!"

"Yes, meaning you. You blink, they win. It's as simple as that."

Slumping onto the couch, Agnes dropped her head into her hands.

"I've been beaten, stabbed, and raped. I don't want any more of this."

Cindy sat down next to Agnes and wrapped an arm around her shoulders.

"Listen to me. There's no way you can lose this if you stay strong. We're going after the city, the state, Ranger Lovejoy, Captain Gonzales, the warden, the mayor and everyone else involved in what happened to you. I may even go after the judges that prolonged your arraignment."

"I don't want Captain Gonzales involved in this. He didn't do anything wrong."

"Maybe not, but the more we include the better chance we have of winning. He's not without blame here, Agnes. A seasoned law enforcement officer should have known better than to be railroaded by a Texas Ranger with an agenda."

"He had no idea what—"

"That's not the point. He's a professional." Cindy shifted and knelt in front of Agnes. "Look at me. Do you trust me?"

Agnes raised her head and stared into Cindy's eyes for several seconds.

"Yes," she finally said.

"Say it."

"I…I trust you."

"Good, because I have never been so sure in my life about a case…but **only** if you hang in there. These people aren't fools. They'll beat you down emotionally and mentally if they can, but they'll never let this go to trial. The publicity and political fallout would be devastating to everyone's career."

"Okay." Agnes's hands began to shake. Cindy clasped them between hers and squeezed.

"Good girl."

†

Agnes stooped and picked up a flat rock from the grassy bank and tossed it sidearm into the lake. The rock skipped along the surface three times before disappearing beneath the smooth water. The crunch of gravel under car tires carried down to the lakeshore signaling that someone else had arrived at the cabin. Agnes searched the ground for another rock. Whoever had come to visit would eventually find their way down to the lake if they were looking for her.

Selecting another stone from her arsenal she half-heartedly made another throw. She frowned as it made an awkward hop and sank a few yards in front of her. For her third attempt she threw her entire weight behind the throw, achieving seven skips.

"Good one, Mom."

Agnes nearly dropped the other rocks she was holding at the sound of her son's voice.

"I've had some time to practice." She threw another. "I thought you weren't coming. You didn't call or write." She felt her son come to a stop beside her.

"Yeah, I should have called, but I was working a few things out. Besides cell phones don't work out here, remember?" Agnes slid a glance over her son. Like his father, he had dark wavy hair. His blue eyes glistened with checked tears as he smiled tentatively at her. She dropped the remaining rocks and wrapped her arms around him, letting go of the months of separation and despair. "I'm so sorry, Mom," Matthew said.

Tears streamed down Agnes's cheeks as she buried her face in his shoulder. How long they stood like that she didn't know but eventually she found the strength to push him away.

"How long are you staying?"

"A couple of days. I can't miss too many classes. Dad packed me a bag and made me drive his truck. I think he just wanted to drive my Mustang." Matthew kicked at a large rock imbedded in the sand. "He said you were selling the house and moving up here."

Agnes wiped her face on the sleeves of her jacket and looked up the hill at the small cabin.

"Yeah. It's peaceful here. Quiet."

Matthew shoved his hands into his jeans pockets.

"I guess Dad and I'll have to do a room addition so I don't have to sleep on that awful couch."

Agnes lightly slapped his shoulder.

"Since when has that ever bothered you?"

"Since I grew a foot taller and a lot wider," Matthew said then smiled. "Or haven't you noticed?"

"I noticed. I'll talk to Griff about it."

"Cool." Matthew fell silent as he looked back at the lake. "Dad says you're still having a pretty rough time. I wish I could have been there for you. Is there anything I can do to help?"

"You already have. Nana's not going to like that you're ignoring her wishes."

"I'm an adult now. She doesn't like most of things I do." Matthew looked sheepishly at the ground.

"I can imagine. You hungry?" Agnes asked, deciding to change the subject.

"Am I breathing?" Matthew asked, throwing his arms out away from his sides.

"Great! Let's go see what's in the fridge." Agnes hooked her arm in Matthew's and began the walk up the hill. "Have you heard from your sister?"

"She's with Nana."

"Ah," Agnes replied. "Is she okay?"

"She's an asshole. Nana, I mean. Sis is fine. A little confused, but Dad's going to talk to her this weekend and then try to talk some sense into Nana."

"Oh Lord," Agnes muttered. If there were ever two people on the earth that should never cross paths it was Griff Elliott and her mother. "I'm glad I'm here."

"Me too, Mom."

Agnes smiled.

Maybe things would be okay, she thought.

"Listen, Matthew, Cindy was here earlier. The city wants to go to trial on my lawsuit. If that happens things will get ugly."

"I'm with you all the way."

"Thank you."

Chapter 29

When the call came in about a body found in Odessa, Cochetta knew they were on the right trail. The problem was it didn't make her feel any better. Phoning Jeff she asked if he could fly back up with her to view the victim. He agreed as long as Captain Gonzales didn't object.

Cochetta was grateful for the company. The stress was taking its toll.

"God I hope this is the last," she muttered after hanging up.

✝

"Another!" Cochetta held up her shot glass and waved it at the bartender. She was well beyond drunk, headed for blissful oblivion. A large shadow fell over her and the booth she was sitting in.

"You've had enough," the bartender said sternly.

Cochetta blinked at the man, her vision blurred from the alcohol she had already consumed. She tilted her head to the side enjoying the light-headed rush.

"Am I still conscious?"

"Barely. Give me a number and I'll call someone to pick you up?"

"I don't know anyone in…" Cochetta looked perplexed then asked, "Where are we?"

"Odessa."

"Oh, right. Victim…" Cochetta held up her hand, flicking her fingers as she tried to count how many women had died so far. "Fuck it! They aren't—" The Ranger burped. "Scuze me… numbers.

Listen here, bartender, I'm not…drunk enough yet." She held up her empty glass. "One more for the road."

"As far as this place is concerned you've had too much. You have two choices. Walk out of here on your own, or get escorted out by the cops. I'm not getting sued because you end up in an accident after you leave here."

Cochetta snarled and threw the shot glass over the bartender's head. It smashed into the long ornate mirror behind the counter. Glass shelves shattered, dropping bottles of liquor onto the floor.

"I want another!"

It took the burly bartender and two other patrons to subdue Cochetta. She was still struggling under the three of them when deputies arrived and cuffed her. One found her ID and laughed.

"Hey, I recognize this woman. She's Cochetta Lovejoy, boys. The superdyke Ranger who had a cop falsely arrested in Ft. Worth for being the Rapture Killer. Word has it she's up here investigating another murder…like we aren't smart enough to do it ourselves." The man reached down and pulled Cochetta's long hair, forcing her face up. "Or should I say the not-so-great Ranger Lovejoy?"

Cochetta heard the mocking laughter.

"Fucking asshole," she growled, twisting her head sideways in an attempt to dislodge the deputy's grip. The pain only agitated her more. When she felt her head yanked backward she spat on the shirt inches away from his face. "Take these cuffs off me and let's see how—"

"Bitch! You might think being a Ranger makes you special but you're nothing but a drunken cunt as far as I'm concerned."

The slap that followed was nothing compared to what happened next. The deputy cursed as he flipped her over and pulled her T-shirt over her head to prevent her from spitting on anything or anyone else.

"You have the right to remain silent, Ranger," he advised, yanking her upward. Even drunk Cochetta felt the pain of her arms being wrenched backward. She kicked at his crotch in retaliation but missed. Another slap snapped her head sideways. Disoriented she slumped falling against the other deputy, knocking him into a table.

"Jesus Christ, Kenny. Knock the bitch out if you have to."

The two deputies finally managed to get a solid grip on her and dragged her to the waiting cruiser. Cochetta braced her feet against the ledge of the car's door. One officer knocked her in the back of her knees with his flashlight causing them to buckle. Forcing her into the back, they slammed the door shut.

"I'd hate to fight her when she's sober," Kenny said. "Damn bitch is mean."

Cochetta slumped forward to rest her head on the cage. Everything after that was a blur.

†

Jeff could hardly believe he was walking into the Odessa County jail to retrieve a Texas Ranger. As a member of her investigative team he had certain responsibilities but bailing his boss out of jail wasn't one of them.

Lovejoy had been unusually quiet on the plane and somewhat distant after they had reviewed the file of the newest body. Both agreed the woman was a Rapture victim.

Leaving the Ranger at her motel room door earlier in the evening, Jeff retired to his own to study his notes. When his phone rang at two a.m., he muttered a few profanities about a little peace and quiet. It didn't help hearing that Lovejoy had been arrested for public intoxication and disorderly conduct.

He approached the information desk cautiously.

"I'm here for Cochetta Lovejoy."

"Ah yes. I'll be happy to let you have her for the bargain price of five thousand dollars," the desk sergeant said with a smile.

"What the fuck did she do, piss in a cruiser?" Jeff asked as he pulled out his wallet and searched for his emergency platinum card.

"I wish. We could tack on more charges and up the bail even higher. It's not every day we have a Texas Ranger as a guest in our motel. She should consider herself lucky she's getting out so soon.

Professional courtesy, you know." The deputy laid out a series of documents for Jeff to sign.

Jeff read the list of infractions and shook his head. A large envelope landed on top of the desk with a thump. The detective looked up at the jailer.

"No gun?"

"Nope. Just her ID and sixty-three dollars and thirty-five cents." He picked up Jeff's credit card and turned away.

Jeff opened the envelope and pulled out the ID wallet and frowned.

"Where's her badge?"

The deputy turned back to him.

"I logged in what was on her. She didn't have a badge." He tapped the credit card receipt with a pen. "Sign this and I'll have her brought out."

Jeff signed the receipt and took his copy. He flipped the little yellow slip of paper over and jotted down the two arresting deputies' names listed on the report. He would be paying them a visit later. Copies of the documents were folded and placed in an envelope. The jailer leaned across the desk giving it to Jeff.

"She'll be coming through there," he said, pointing toward a brown door. "When she sobers up tell her she's getting a bill from the bar too. Have a nice morning."

Jeff turned away from the desk in time to see Lovejoy pushed through the door, followed by another man. Even before she got near him he could smell urine and vomit.

"God, the rental company is going to charge us extra just because of the stench. You're paying for it."

Lovejoy growled and stomped away.

"Assholes!" she spat out before turning back to Jeff. "Took your time, Detective."

"You're damn lucky I'm here at all. This isn't part of my job description…and you owe me five grand. Now, if you're done entertaining the locals, maybe we can get back to the hotel. You need a shower and I need sleep." He turned and walked out. It was up to Lovejoy to follow him or not.

†

Cochetta felt like a she had been dragged a mile over an old, bumpy, pothole-riddled road. She rolled out of bed, feeling sick and disoriented. It probably wouldn't have been so bad except she landed in the discarded pile of clothes she had worn the night before. The smell sent her stomach into spasms. She barely made it to the toilet. The next half hour was spent hugging the porcelain bowl.

Wiping her mouth she stared into the mirror trying to recollect the previous evening's events. Foggy images faded in and out.

"Shit!" she muttered, bending her head to splash water on her face and then wincing as a pain shot up the right side. Cochetta lifted her shirt and turned her left side toward the mirror. A large purplish-blue bruise covered most of her ribs. "Well, you certainly were on the losing end of something last night," she muttered to her reflection and grimaced.

Ugh! Shower time. Instead of taking one when she got back to her room, she had fallen straight into bed. The maids weren't going to appreciate cleaning up after her today.

Chapter 30

Being on a statewide jurisdiction task force had several advantages. Jeff had no trouble gaining access to the two deputies who had arrested Cochetta. A call to their supervisor identifying himself and requesting a midmorning meeting ensured he'd be accommodated. After that it was only a matter of explaining about the political ramifications of the missing badge. The Texas Rangers wouldn't look kindly on its theft.

"I'm sure we can keep all of this between us, Sgt. Hanson," Jeff said, casually leaning back in his chair. "Ranger Lovejoy may not even know it's gone yet, and well, if the deputies simply return it, I doubt if she's going to make an issue of it."

The sergeant agreed. The last thing he needed was the sheriff coming down on him because two of his men had fucked up. Grabbing the phone he dialed the dispatcher's office.

"Call White and Peterson in here." After a long pause he raised his voice. "I don't care if they just got off duty. I want them in my office in twenty minutes and if I have to I'll send someone to personally escort them here!" Slamming the phone down, he shook his head. "Those two are going to get the department sued one day. You want another cup?" he asked Jeff, pointing toward a small coffeepot on a file cabinet against the wall.

"Thanks."

✝

Carl White epitomized the clichéd image of a redneck. He was foolhardy, rude, and cocky; a combination that Jeff detested, especially in a police officer. When he and Peterson swaggered into their sergeant's office, they glanced uninterestedly at Jeff and then turned to Hanson.

"What's up, Sarge? Kenny and I, we had a hard night and want to get something to eat before heading home."

Glaring, Sgt. Hanson stood up.

"White, if either of you ever enter my office again without knocking I'll write you up for insubordination. I'm tired of you two yahoos causing me trouble."

Holding up his hands White backed up a step.

"Whoa now, Sarge. What's got you so riled up? We're just tired, ain't we, Kenny?" Peterson nodded but didn't say anything. "No disrespect intended."

"Good!" Pointing toward Jeff without breaking eye contact with White. "This is Detective Roberts. He's from the task force assigned to the Rapture Killer investigation…an investigation led by Texas Ranger Lovejoy."

White smirked and turned toward the detective.

"Oh yeah, the bitch we arrested last night. She showed up all high and mighty to investigate a crime scene. Like we can't do the job. Turns out she's nothing but a drunk…a mean one at that. Tore up a bar and resisted arrest. Fought Kenny and I all the way to the car. Even had the nerve to spit on me, so if you're here to ask us to drop the charges against her it ain't going to happen. Right Kenny?"

"Right," Kenny said. "We have her dead to right, drunk and disorderly, resisting arrest, assault. Her pretty little ass is—"

"Shut up!" Sgt. Hanson said, clearly on the verge of losing his temper. "You two are staying here while I go for a walk. I strongly suggest for your own good you listen to what Detective Roberts has to say." Pushing past the two deputies, Hanson slammed the door behind him.

"We said we aren't—" White began.

Jeff prided himself on being a man of even temper. Words were often his best weapon. At the moment, though, he didn't give a damn about appearance and perception.

"You don't listen well, do you White? Sgt. Hanson already told you to shut up, so shut up!" White's mouth clamped shut. "You two are a couple of pathetic, ignorant pieces of shit and I know exactly what to do with shit."

"You can't talk…" Peterson piped in.

"I can talk to you any way I want and you know why? Because both of you are about to be arrested for theft."

"You're fuckin' crazy! Just like that Lovejoy bitch!"

"I'm not going to tell you again to shut up. If I call Sgt. Hanson back in I'll file charges against both of you for stealing Ranger Lovejoy's badge. That's a felony that will land both of you in jail for several years. That's state property."

Peterson looked anxiously at his partner.

"I told you not to take that," he said. His voice quivered nervously.

"Shut up, Kenny." Turning to Detective Roberts, he attempted a friendly smile but failed. "Listen…umm…Roberts, isn't it?"

"Detective Roberts."

"Right, Detective Roberts. We didn't steal anything. We just wanted to make sure it didn't get lost or taken by someone as a souvenir. You know how that is sometimes. Here," he said, fishing it out of his shirt pocket and tossing it on the desk.

"It's not that simple," Jeff said.

"You can't prove anything."

"Sure I can. You didn't turn it in when you brought Ranger Lovejoy to the jail. That alone is enough to get you fired. The fact that you're off duty now and left the premises with it makes it theft. Of course, there is a way out of this—"

"How?" White asked, willing to jump at anything if it got him and Peterson off the hook.

"Drop the charges against Lovejoy and we'll call it even."

"That bitch…"

Jeff gave him a warning look.

"What's it to be, White? She may lose her job over this if she's convicted but I doubt if she'll spend any more time in jail. You two, however, will spend a few years. The State doesn't take kindly to law enforcement officers that steal. I'm offering you a way out. Drop the charges and it ends here. Everybody gets to keep their job. This all is just a big misunderstanding."

"What about the arrest report? We can't change that."

"You figure it out." Jeff picked up the badge, threw his business card on the desk and walked to the door. "File something saying you learned she'd been drugged. I'm sure you can dig up a few witnesses to back you up. Your type can always find someone who's good at lying. I'm going to get something to eat. If I don't hear from you by the time I'm finished I'll file my report. Then it will be too late. Oh…one more thing." White and Peterson looked warily at the detective. "If I hear that either of you mother fuckers have disparaged Ranger Lovejoy in any way I will *personally* have your asses hung out to dry. Now you have a good day!" Opening the door, Jeff stepped into the outer office. Sgt. Hanson was talking with another deputy. "They're all yours, Sgt. Hanson. Thank you for your cooperation."

"Any time, Detective."

✝

After grabbing a bite to eat, Jeff spent the rest of the day at the local police department viewing several DVDs he had brought on the trip to Odessa. They were from security cameras deployed at businesses in and around the areas near where each of the victims had been found. Doing something was better than nothing while he waited to hear from Lovejoy. Finally, bored, he called her cell phone. On the third attempt she answered.

"What?" an angry voice demanded.

"Well, it's good to know you're still alive," he said sarcastically. "Are you coming in to work or going to take the rest of the day off?"

"Go to hell!" Lovejoy growled.

"Been there, done that! So are you coming in or not?"

"I'll be there." The phone clicked.

Jeff looked at his phone and grimaced. He actually hoped she decided not to come in. The last thing he needed was a hung over Texas Ranger on his hands.

Chapter 31

Cochetta sat in front of a small monitor watching the same DVDs Jeff had viewed earlier in the day. When she arrived at the police station she was informed that Detective Roberts had gone out but would be back shortly. The officer led her to a room they had made available for his use.

"Fucking headache!" she muttered, leaning forward to rub her eyes. "Fucking damn case!" Nothing in the videos was of help, but with the headache she could be missing something. The sound of something thudding on the desk in front of her startled her. Her head snapped up. Pain shot through her temples.

"Damn it!"

"Your stuff from last night," Jeff said as he sank into a chair against the wall. "I hope you stashed your gun in your room before you made an ass out of yourself."

Cochetta pulled back the right side of her jean jacket to reveal the revolver's handle at her hip.

"I'm not a complete idiot." She dumped out the contents of the envelope and sighed in relief as her ID flopped open along with her badge. She had torn the motel room apart searching for them. Being arrested was nothing compared to losing her badge. "Thanks. At least I won't have to deal with that when I get recalled."

"Recalled? For being drugged?"

Deputy White had decided to cooperate. Not surprising.

"Drugged? I wasn't—"

"Sure you were. The arresting deputies just filed a supplemental report. Several witnesses came forward stating they saw something being slipped into one of your drinks."

"That's crazy! No one—"

"Drop it, Lovejoy. Consider yourself lucky this time. I don't know what your department will say about this, but you won't be losing your job. It's not against the rules to have a few drinks in a bar when you're off duty."

Confused, Cochetta shook her head. Nothing made sense.

"I don't know what to say."

"Well, the first thing is when you'll be paying me the five thousand bucks I posted for you. I want that off my credit card as soon as possible. And any other fees I'm stuck with. I think that's considered a cash advance and the interest rates suck."

"Tomorrow. I'll have it to you tomorrow," she said, massaging her temples.

Jeff cursed himself and pulled his chair forward.

"Cochetta, you need to take some time off. You're not doing anyone any good like this."

"Like what?" Cochetta spat.

"Like a truck heading toward a cliff!" Jeff hissed. "You've been on this case for almost six months without a break. You're taking sleeping pills and now you got yourself arrested for drunk and disorderly, not to mention resisting arrest. The next time…"

"There won't be a next time. I'm not giving up even if it takes me another six months!" Cochetta turned back to the monitor. "I'm missing something here," she said. "I know it."

"You're too stubborn for your own good."

Cochetta ignored him. The minutes and seconds ticked off on the bottom of the screen as she stared at the moving images.

"Back it up," Jeff said, leaning forward. She looked at him. "Back it up!" Jeff repeated. "Look. The victim was found in front of the gazebo by the Meadowbrook clubhouse. Whoever dropped her off would have had to approach from…there!" Jeff pointed to a dark car moving slowly along the edge of a parking lot. The lights on the vehicle were off. Trees partially obscured the view.

She looked at the bottom of the screen. "Hmmm, 3:23 a.m. Are there other security cameras installed facing the entrance to the course?"

Jeff dipped into a small box beside the table and pulled out several more disks.

Cochetta ejected the one she was watching and marked it with a sticky note before inserting another and fast-forwarding it to the approximate time period.

"Gotcha! You aren't as smart as you think," she exclaimed. The rear image of the same car was captured leaving the parking lot. "We need to get back to Ft. Worth."

✝

Jeff and Cochetta stood behind a dark blue Chevy Malibu that was parked in space twenty-five of the parking garage. Several images on the vehicle had been captured and enlarged making it possible to read the license plate. It belonged to a business named Torres Enterprises.

"Okay..." The office manager walked up to them shuffling some paperwork. "Mr. Torres signed for the car on those dates."

"Keys?" Cochetta held her hand out.

"I'm waiting for him to give me auth—"

Jeff shook his head.

"Mr. Fernando, we believe this car was involved in a murder. It's going to be towed whether Torres gives his permission or not. Now we can do this the easy way or we can do it the hard way. The easy way makes you and the company look good. You know...cooperative. Tell Mr. Torres I said that and that we'll be wanting to talk to him."

The manager reluctantly held out the keys.

Cochetta grabbed them and motioned to a waiting tow truck. She pulled on a pair of latex gloves and opened the trunk of the car.

"Just a quick look."

Jeff nodded and pulled on his own gloves before opening the driver's side door. The inside appeared clean. He walked around to the back of the car and peered in the trunk.

"Someone is good at cleaning up," he said.

"There are some stains, here. Hopefully forensics will get something useable from them." Cochetta shut the trunk.

"But maybe not so good at cover-up. This was her second big mistake. Let's see if we can get in to see Mr. Torres. Know anything about him?"

"Hector Torres? Most people in this area know his name. He's a pretty prominent guy, wealthy, served three terms on city council."

Cochetta said, checking her watch. "If we hurry we may be able to catch Torres at his office."

"Worth a try," Jeff replied. Cochetta sat quietly while he drove. "Something bothering you?" he asked, after a long silence.

"I was just thinking about Elliott. Is she okay?"

Jeff shook his head.

"We don't talk about Agnes." He pulled his seat belt snug against his thighs.

"People make mistakes," Cochetta said defensively.

Jeff scoffed then turned to look at her.

"Yes they do. The problem with you, Lovejoy, is that you can't admit you're one of those people. Can you even fathom what she's been through? What she's lost?" Cochetta shook her head. "I didn't think so. Get this straight! You and I, we work together, nothing more. Agnes is off limits."

Turning her head, Cochetta stared at the passing buildings. There was nothing she could say to change what had happened. More women had died because she had been too focused on Elliott. It was true the detective had suffered but she was strong. She'd survive it. Those dead women, well…Cochetta settled back into her own seat. They had another new lead. As slim as it was, it was something.

Chapter 32

Marcella was having a hard time listening to her client. The gym was small but had a long list of loyal patrons. She had visited the facilities several times, occasionally tweaking the older equipment. The last time she made a proposal to the owner for a few upgrades. Now all she had to do was finish sealing the deal. Unfortunately, she was distracted by a small, muscular blonde working on a circuit training routine.

Now isn't the time, she scolded herself.

"She's cute, huh?" the owner said, handing her a check.

"Pardon?"

"The girl! Her name's Brat. She's a regular. I can introduce you if you want."

Marcella blushed and rubbed the back of her neck.

"I don't think—"

"Have I read you wrong? You do like women, don't you?"

Marcella bit her lower lip.

"No. I mean yes. No, you aren't wrong," she admitted softly.

"Then let me introduce you. She's a great kid!"

Marcella's brain raced.

"Sure…Okay," she said, her face turning even redder. *Just for drinks. Maybe dinner*, she told herself. *Maybe I can do this. I don't have to kill every one of them. We could just be friends. He didn't say I couldn't have a friend. If there's no sex there's no sin.* Marcella tried to make herself believe those words.

✝

Marcella took several calming breaths before entering the Fruit Jar later that day. Wanda had wanted to introduce her to Brat in a more relaxed environment. The interior was not as dark as she expected, and much cleaner. She kept her eyes down as she walked to the bar.

"Marcy!"

Marcella cringed. She hated the shortened version of her name. Wanda Jenkins, the gym owner, was sitting at the bar holding a beer.

"I almost gave up hope on you. Sit! What do you want to drink?"

"I almost didn't come," Marcella admitted, taking the offered seat. Glancing around the room she saw two men in a booth kissing. *Sinners*, she thought, wishing she could send them straight to hell. Men weren't worth saving.

"You're not getting cold feet on me are you?" Wanda asked.

Marcella shook her head.

"No. It's just…"

Wanda patted her hand kindly.

"I understand. Don't worry. Brat doesn't gossip."

"Why do you call her Brat?"

"Oh, she can be a real pain in the ass sometimes!" The woman behind the bar guffawed.

Marcella stared wide-eyed at the bartender.

"Hi! I'm Telly. You must be Marcy. Wanda's told me all about you. So you're gonna take my little Brat out tonight?"

Marcella swallowed.

"Your little brat?"

"Not literally. We're all fond of her here so we're a bit protective."

"Oh…well…my intentions…"

"Your intentions? My goodness, Wanda, I believe we have a civilized woman here." Telly slapped the bar with a wet towel and chuckled as Marcella jumped. Marcella smiled thinly.

"Telly quit teasing and go get Brat. You're making Marcy nervous," Wanda said good-naturedly. She laughed as the bartender put on a dramatic pout and turned toward the kitchen door. Wanda leaned close to Marcella. "Don't let Telly scare you. She likes to pull everyone's leg a bit. A lot of bark and no bite, unless provoked."

Marcella nodded. Wanda's words didn't keep her from feeling nervous but she was hopeful. *Tonight will be different. Brat isn't like the others.*

Wanting to give Marcy and Brat a bit of privacy Telly motioned at Wanda to join her at the other end of the bar.

"She's not bad looking," Telly said, nodding toward Marcy.

"Marcy's nice. A little quiet but smart as a whip."

"You know her for long?"

Wanda shrugged. "Awhile. She services our equipment. I think she's a little lonely though. Brat will be good for her."

"Brat's good for everyone, but she's a bit naïve. Thanks for bringing Marcy here. At least meeting her makes me feel better. With all these murders taking place…" Telly hesitated, thinking about the artist's drawing the detective had shown her. *If it wasn't for the blond hair, she does resemble…* Shaking her head, the bartender frowned.

"What?" Wanda asked.

"Nothing. So, you want another drink? On me, this time," Telly offered.

"Fill her up!"

Chapter 33

Brat struggled against the bonds that held her firmly in place. She didn't know where she was or remember what had happened after leaving the bar with Marcy. The entire evening was wiped from her memory. Her mouth felt dry. A blindfold covered her eyes making it impossible to see. Groaning, she tried shifting her position.

"You're awake," a woman's voice said. "I thought maybe I gave you too much."

Brat's head jerked to the left.

"Marcy? What happened? Were we in an accident?"

"No. I'm sorry, Brat. I really didn't want this to happen. I like you. You're so innocent. You shouldn't ever trust people on first dates, you know." Marcella thought about the hitchhiker. She was too trusting too. Young girls today were ridiculously naïve. "I couldn't believe it when you agreed to go to my place. I thought you were different from the others."

"Your place? Is this your apartment?"

"No. I don't even live in the area."

"How? I mean what happened to me? I feel…weird."

Marcella laughed.

"You don't remember us stopping for a couple of hamburgers after we left the bar? Oh, Brat, you're priceless. I wish you had just wanted to be friends. We could have, you know."

"I don't understand."

"Sure you do. You want to have sex with me."

"I just said I'd go back to your place for a while. You didn't say anything about sex," Brat said, tugging at her restraints.

"You want it. When I realized you are like the others, I spiked your Coke while you were in the restroom. By the time we got back to my car you were out of it."

"Please. I honestly thought we were just going to have a few drinks. Nothing more. What do you want?" A plastic straw was pressed between her lips.

"Here, have a drink. Not too much. It might make you sick."

Brat cautiously sucked a small amount of liquid into her mouth and was relieved that it was only water…at least she hoped. She took several deep sips and then turned her head to the side indicating she'd had enough.

"Marcy, why am I tied up?"

"I hate that name," Marcella said, slamming the water bottle down.

"I'm sorry. I didn't know. Everyone was calling you that. You didn't say anything when I called you that earlier."

"That's because I like you. I didn't want to seem too standoffish. My name is Marcella."

"Please, Marcella, I want to go home," Brat said softly, her voice shaking. The bed she was strapped down to dipped beside her and a latex gloved hand stroked her cheek.

"You will," Marcella said kindly. "After we're done. Maybe you're not like the others."

"Others?"

"Yeah! Those whores. You're not a whore…are you?"

"N…no."

"Good, because if you were—"

"I'm not a whore, Marc…Marcella. Honest!"

"I know. That's why I'm going to let you go after you repent your sins."

"Repent?"

"Yes. Confess your sins. I can give you penance," Marcella explained as her hand wandered down the center of Brat's chest to rest on her stomach. "God granted me that power. If you tell me about your sins He'll forgive you. Then we can plan our future. I have champagne chilling."

"I don't understand."

"Your **sins!**" Marcella hissed. Her patience was beginning to wane. "You don't want to burn in hell do you?"

"I…I don't believe in God or hell. Please, I just want to go home!" Brat's head snapped sideways as the gloved hand struck her hard across her left cheek and lips. Blood trickled down her chin from a split.

"You're an **atheist**?" Marcella screamed, feeling an unimaginable disgust. She couldn't grant penance to a nonbeliever. "You deny Jesus, Our Lord, as the savior?"

"I…I…" Terrified, Brat began to cry.

"You stupid, ignorant woman!" Marcella pounced on Brat's prone body, straddling her hips. "You can't be an atheist," she yelled, slapping Brat again. "Why are you lying to me? I can't be friends with an atheist."

"I'm so sorry."

"Sorry? I wasn't going to kill you. All you had to do was repent and I would have let you go. You're worse than those whores. At least they understood they were sinners."

"You're her…you're the Rapture—"

"Don't call me that! I'm not a killer. I'm a deliverer." Marcella smiled. "An atheist! You're going to be my best gift yet. When you realize how wrong you've been you'll thank me for saving you." The knife lay on a white towel on the nightstand by the bed. Marcella looked at it almost lovingly.

†

The cold water from the shower looked and smelled like rust. The motel had been closed several weeks, scheduled for major renovations. Fortunately for Marcella, the city was making it difficult for the owner to get the proper permits. Although the power was off to discourage squatters, the water was still on. Whether it was an oversight or left on for when the renovations could be started wasn't important. Being able to clean up was all that mattered.

Marcella spent more than twenty minutes under the stream of water scrubbing the blood from her skin. After drying off with a towel she'd brought, she slipped into her clothes. Fully dressed, Marcella picked up the single candle that had illuminated the room and a black garbage bag, carrying both into the main room.

Two candles burned on the dresser. On the floor was the plastic bundled body of Brat. All that was left to do was load the body into her trunk and locate an appropriate dumpsite.

"I really didn't want to do this. I thought you were different," Marcella mumbled, standing over the body. "You should have believed in God. Then you could have repented. I'd have let you go. All you had to do was believe." The sad irony was that Marcella honestly believed what she was saying. In her mind she pictured Brat confessing her sins and begging for forgiveness. Marcella would have been merciful. God told her she could be merciful when she first laid eyes on Brat. Why else would she have risked everything by letting Wanda arrange the meeting? And there was Telly. The two women knew who she was. They'd be able to identify her. "What have I done?" Collapsing into the chair by the boarded up window, she grabbed her hair and began shaking her head. "Wanda has my phone number. I have to think of something."

Why did this have to happen, God? You knew she didn't believe in you. That's it, isn't it? That's why you sent her to me. This was another test! Haven't I proven my worth? How many more women do you want? When will I be free of this? I'm so lonely.

Marcella had given Brat several opportunities to be born again in Christ but the woman had refused. Cut after cut, the gift was offered and rejected until it was too late. When Brat finally begged Marcella to tell her what to say her injuries were so severe Marcella couldn't save her…at least in this world.

Staring down at the lifeless body she felt enormous sadness.

It's your fault. You made me do it. Why did you have to be so stubborn? You didn't have to die.

†

Marcella flung the plastic bag and her kit in the backseat of the car. Getting Brat into the trunk was going to be difficult but she had handled bodies before. First she had to move the vehicle closer to the door. Sliding behind the wheel, she reached for the ignition when a flash of headlights on the side of the motel caused her heart to leap in her chest. She bent sideways making sure her feet didn't touch the brake pedal. Eventually the light faded. Peeking over the dash she scanned the area looking for anyone or anything that might be in the area. With the coast clear she sat up and started the engine. Slowly inching it backward she stopped when she saw the flicker of red and blue lights at the far end of the motel. Panicking she shifted into drive, pressed the gas pedal and sped away. Her heart pounded painfully. Her ears roared with the sound of rushing blood.

Glancing nervously at the rearview mirror she glimpsed a black state trooper vehicle easing around the corner of the motel, shining a spotlight on the exterior. Apparently the officer hadn't seen her leaving. Not wanting to chance being stopped by another cop Marcella decided to spend the night in a motel.

†

She was so tired. Brat wasn't supposed to die. She was different from the others.

She was an atheist, the voice said.

Only at first, Marcella replied. *I changed her but it was too late.*

You did change her. The voice laughed. *She'll never be the same, will she?*

Pressing her palms against her ears, Marcella tried to muffle the sound. The ringing of her cell phone was the only thing that silenced the laughter. It was Hector.

The police wanted to talk to her. Why, he couldn't say since they were still in his office. He suggested she meet with them.

"Bring your lawyer," he said before hanging up. Hector liked to keep things tidy. Attorneys were good at that.

Sweet, naive, Hector. No one knew him like she did. He was tough in business but weak when it came to her. She could get him to agree to almost anything. He wanted to marry Marcella. She promised to consider it knowing it would be a marriage of convenience. The man was impotent which suited her fine. The thought of having a man's dick inside her was revolting. Marcella's head dropped into her hands. *How much longer must I do your work? I can't sleep, I can't eat. Every day you ask more and more. Will this ever end? Haven't I proven myself?*

No, the voice replied, laughing louder than before. *No.*

Chapter 34

"Listen, Jeff, there's no reason for us to be fighting like this," Cochetta said, finally breaking the silence. "We both want the same thing so let's put our differences aside and do our jobs."

"I always do my job," Jeff replied, coolly.

"I didn't mean it like that and you know it. Let's just change the subject. What else do you know about Torres?"

"I've heard he can be a real asshole when he wants to be. He pushes people around like they are pawns on a chessboard," Jeff said as he and Cochetta stepped off the elevator that delivered them to the twenty-sixth floor of a downtown office building in Dallas.

"We should get along quite well, then," Cochetta said dryly. She stopped in front of a large desk blocking a beautifully carved wooden door. An older woman with wire-framed glasses was flipping through a folder.

"We're here to see Mr. Torres."

"Do you have an appointment?" The receptionist asked, not bothering to look up from her paperwork.

"Actually we have something better. Badges," Jeff said, lowering his ID in front of her face.

The woman took off her wire-framed glasses, folding them slowly before glancing up at Jeff and Cochetta.

"I'll see if he's in. You can have a seat over there." She motioned to a small waiting area to her right. Picking up the phone she dialed a number.

"She certainly looks the part," Cochetta said.

"The part?"

"Yeah, the efficient, unruffled, personal secretary."

Before Jeff could answer the receptionist called out.

"Please follow me." She stood and came around the desk, leading them down a long wide hallway.

Jeff leaned over toward Cochetta and whispered, "You're right. Just like in the movies."

The conference room was empty.

"Mr. Torres will be in shortly," the woman said and left.

"I guess that means we should make ourselves at home," Jeff said.

Minutes later, a tall Hispanic man in a gray suit walked in. His salt-and-pepper hair was neatly trimmed, as was the mustache and goatee.

"I am Mr. Torres. I assume you are the officers who had my car impounded. What can I do for you?" Torres's deep, rich voice had a faint accent.

"You signed out one of your fleet cars to someone. We'd like to know to whom?"

"I sign cars out all the time. I don't believe that's illegal. As you said I have an entire fleet of vehicles."

"Mr. Torres, I know your branch manager called you about the vehicle we're talking about," Jeff said as he walked behind Hector Torres, deliberately taking the long way back to have a seat next to Cochetta. He noticed that Torres's left hand was slightly clenched.

"He did. I understand you coerced him into giving you the keys. Not very smart on your part, nor his, but for the sake of cooperation I'll give you the opportunity to explain before I call my lawyer."

"We appreciate your cooperation, Mr. Torres. We simply want the name of the woman you loaned the car to," Jeff said as he flipped open his notepad.

"I don't believe I said it was a woman."

"Well, *his* name then."

Hector looked at his watch and then pulled a cell phone from his pocket without looking at Cochetta or Jeff.

"I never said it was a him either. Before I give you any information I'll need the person's permission."

"I'd rather you not make that call," Cochetta said, reaching over to cover it with her hand.

Startled, Hector looked up and then jerked his hand away.

"I believe this conversation is over," he said, turning to leave.

"One moment, Mr. Torres…please," Cochetta said. Using her own cell she quickly thumbed in a number. "Lou, would you call Judge Alvarez and get me a warrant for Hector Torres's office, cell and home phone numbers for the last six months. Probable cause? A vehicle in his fleet in Laredo is involved in a murder. Thanks."

Jeff leaned forward on the table, resting his elbows on the smooth polished wood. His attention was focused completely on Hector Torres's left hand, which had dropped to his side. It was clenching and unclenching nervously.

Cochetta snapped her phone shut and tucked it back in her pocket.

"You can make that call now. We'll have the number within an hour or you can give it to us now."

"Like I said, I'll have to ask permission. My phone records won't do you any good. I'll simply use one of my employee's phones. Your warrant won't extend to them, no matter what judge you have in your pocket. Now if you'll excuse me, I have a call to make."

"Mr. Torres, when you make that call at least don't disclose what this is about," Cochetta advised. "Unless you want to be considered an accomplice to a murder, after the fact."

Hector frowned.

"Excuse me." Hector dialed a number and walked over to the window, his back to the officers. After a short conversation he turned around.

"My friend has agreed to meet with you as long as she has her attorney present. That would be Mr. Brian Lots. He'll call you to set up the appointment."

"Why an attorney?" Cochetta asked. "Innocent people don't need attorneys."

"You must be joking, Ranger Lovejoy. It *is* Ranger Lovejoy, isn't it? Didn't you recently have a detective arrested and jailed for a crime she didn't commit?"

Cochetta's cheeks burned red.

"This isn't about Ranger Lovejoy, Mr. Torres. Your company's name is on the registration for a vehicle used to transport a murder victim. Give us your friend's name, contact information and we're out of here. If you don't then we have to assume you might be an accessory. I don't think the publicity would be good for your image." Jeff's instincts told him that appearances were very important to Hector Torres. "The media would have a heyday!"

"You certainly present me with a dilemma, Detective. I value my friend very much. On the other hand I don't wish to seem uncooperative," Hector said. "If I provide you with the information you want, would you call off the warrant?"

"That's all we wanted to begin with," Cochetta said, setting her anger aside.

"Fine. Wait here while I pull her file."

"File?" Jeff and Cochetta looked at each other.

"I'm a businessman first, Detective Roberts. Keeping records is a critical part of success. You never know when you might need to know something, even on your friends."

Cochetta glanced at Jeff.

"What do you think?"

"I can't argue with his reasoning. We are asking him for information on a friend. Just don't make any more calls to her," Jeff advised.

Hector smiled and extended his hand to him and then Cochetta.

"I wouldn't think of it. You'll keep me informed? My secretary will have the file ready for you as well as a contact number if you need my assistance again," he said and then left.

†

Jeff stepped outside the room and took a deep breath. This could be the break they needed. Turning he stared thoughtfully at Cochetta for a few moments.

"What?" Cochetta asked, feeling uncomfortable.

"I want you to remove yourself from this case."

"You're crazy! We're on the verge of identifying the killer. I'm not about to turn this over to someone else! I'm too close to closing it."

"We're close, Lovejoy, and that's the problem. You've made all of this about you. Everything could fall apart if you continue as lead investigator. Hell, Torres is right. You arrested the wrong person. The real killer's defense attorney is going to bring that up at trial. That's reasonable doubt about your competency. Do you want the killer to walk just because your ego got in the way?"

"Why are you bringing this up now? If it's about credit for making the arrest…" Cochetta's eyes flashed angrily.

"You know, Cochetta…" Jeff had never called her by her first name before. "The difference between you and me is I don't give a rat's ass who gets the credit. Catching the killer is all that matters. Walk away or at least turn the lead over to someone else."

"No." Cochetta shook her head. "I'll see this through to the end."

Jeff stepped closer to the Ranger and lowered his voice.

"How many more have to die before you get it?"

Cochetta pushed him back.

"You're out of line, Roberts. I'll have your badge for insubordination!"

"You don't have that authority, Lovejoy. I may be assigned to the team but I don't work for you or the Rangers." He turned on his heels and walked away.

"Roberts!"

Jeff pushed through the glass doors of Torres's office building without looking back. He was pissed. The last thing he needed was another confrontation with her. All he wanted was to go home.

"Jeff!"

Ignoring her he headed toward his car. When a hand grabbed his shoulder he spun around.

"Get your hand off me, Lovejoy," he said, knocking it aside.

"You're asking me to do something I can't do. Damn it, I've spent more time on this case than anyone. I have more reason to see it through than anyone," Cochetta said, exasperated.

"No, you don't. You aren't a victim here. You aren't their family or their friend. They deserve the best we can give, and if that means you moving aside then you have an obligation to them to do that."

Before Cochetta could say anything Jeff's phone rang. The expression on his face hardened as he listened to the person on the end. His eyes blazed with anger.

"They found another body in a motel room. Let's go!"

"Jeff—"

"Drop it, Lovejoy. You—"

"Jeff, I'll think about what you've said," Cochetta said.

Jeff held up his hand.

"Drop it! I'm tired, I'm angry and I'm fed up. We have work to do."

✝

The ride to the scene was tense. Neither spoke.

Jeff's stomach lurched as they pulled into the motel's parking lot. He had seen too many bloody bodies in the past months. Ft. Worth had become a killing zone.

Maybe I'm the one who needs the break, he thought, climbing wearily out of his car.

Without saying a word Cochetta stomped away, heading toward a young female officer standing near an open door.

"Is it okay for me to look around?" she asked, showing her badge and ID.

"Sure. They'll be moving the body shortly."

Cochetta carefully entered the room. The smell of blood was strong. Jeff brushed shoulders with her as he entered the room to stand next to her.

"The officer who found her said he noticed the open door a little after two this morning and pulled in to have a closer look. He saw a vehicle speeding away but thought it was more important to check in here. By the time he saw the body the car was gone. He called in a vague description to dispatch but without knowing what direction it was going there wasn't much anyone could do."

Jeff looked around the room and shook his head.

When does it stop?

"Anything else?" Cochetta asked, eyeing the techs who were lifting the bagged body onto a gurney.

"Candlewax remnants, plastic wrap, and the victim's clothes. We also found her ID. Her name is Rebecca O'Quinn...local address. The killer must have been interrupted and panicked."

Cochetta walked to the gurney.

"Mind if we have a look?"

"She's a mess," the aide said as he reached for the zipper.

"They always are," Jeff replied wearily.

The zipper was lowered. Pulling the edges apart he separated the clear plastic to reveal the young woman's face.

"Jesus fucking Christ!" Cochetta swung around, pushing Jeff aside. Clutching her stomach she rushed out the door, barely making it in time before vomiting.

It took Jeff a few seconds longer before he recognized the young woman's cut-up body.

Putting the pieces of flesh together on her face, it dawned on him who she was. God damn it! Why Brat? How? Storming from the room, he kicked at an empty plastic water bottle lying on the floor..

Chapter 35

Lou Chapman leaned against the wall watching and listening to Cochetta as she paced back and forth voicing her anger and frustration. She was clearly on the verge of a breakdown, he thought. Sometimes she yelled. Sometimes she talked rationally, calmly trying to explain what she needed to do. Lou cocked his head to the side waiting for the right moment to speak up.

"Okay, so you're stepping down from the case. Have you told George?"

"Yes and no." Cochetta collapsed into a folding chair. "He suggested I back off and make you the lead investigator."

"And?"

"And I think he's right. It will be less complicated later."

"You mean at the trial."

"Yeah."

"But…"

Cochetta gave Lou a questioning look. "But what?" she asked.

"I've heard a lot about you, Cochetta. You don't give up on anything. If you're stepping down it's strictly for show, which means I'm lead investigator in name only, right?" When she didn't answer, Lou shook his head.

"That's what I thought! I'm not your patsy. If I'm in charge, I'm in charge. You take orders from me."

"As long as you don't screw up I'm fine with that. All I'm interested in is making sure everything looks by the book."

Lou nodded.

"Always covering your butt. You're good at that," Lou said, his voice slightly tinged with sarcasm.

Cochetta jumped to her feet.

"This is about the case!" she replied coldly.

"All right! Sorry!" Lou checked his watch. "Your news conference is in about five minutes."

Cochetta sighed.

"Let's get this over with. From now on I'm just a lackey in the field."

"Is that what you think about everyone under you?" Lou asked, walking away before she could answer.

Chapter 36

Agnes taped the bottom of a box, one of dozens she had put together. The last time her home had been in such disarray was when she and Griff moved into it twenty years ago. In the background the TV droned boringly. She positioned the box next to the long row of shelves that contained books and knickknacks.

She looked up at the TV when the game show suddenly disappeared, replaced by a live news announcement. A reporter was staring into the camera outside the main headquarters of the Ft. Worth Police Department.

"We are interrupting our normally scheduled program with breaking news about the ongoing hunt for the Rapture Killer. Rangers Cochetta Lovejoy and Lou Chapman are about to make an announcement." The camera switched to the two Rangers standing at a podium in the PD conference room. Lovejoy leaned slightly forward toward the microphone.

"Ladies and gentlemen. Thank you for coming on such short notice. At this time I'm announcing that Ranger Chapman will be taking over as lead investigator of the team. Ranger Chapman has been part of the investigative team since the beginning of the year. He is as familiar with the case as I am. All questions should be directed to him."

"Why are you stepping down?" one reporter called out. "Is it because of Detective Kelly-Elliott?"

"Have you caught the Rapture Killer?" another yelled.

Cochetta stepped back from the podium without answering. Ranger Chapman shifted to where she had been standing.

"That's all we have to say for now. Thank you again for your time."

Agnes slumped into the nearest chair and stared at the screen. She didn't know how long she'd been sitting when the phone rang.

"Hello?"

"Are you watching television?"

"Yeah," Agnes said, stunned at the change of events.

"What just happened?" Griff's rough voice asked in bewilderment over the line.

"She stepped down, but she's still on the case."

"This doesn't make sense. Lovejoy isn't a follower," Griff said. Agnes could hear the sound of something rustling in his background.

"What's for dinner?" she asked, knowing he was probably getting ready to microwave a pizza.

"Open the door and find out." The phone line went dead.

Agnes smiled. Walking to the door she flung it open and motioned him in.

"Burger Box!" Griff declared, proudly displaying two bags.

Agnes grabbed one and peeked inside.

"Onion rings! Perfect!" Snatching one she turned and walked into the living room. "Thank you. That was thoughtful." She patted the spot beside her.

"What do you think?" Griff asked.

"I don't know. Maybe she's realized the damage she's done…or it's a ploy. I can't imagine her just turning over the lead to anyone else." Agnes said between bites of burger.

"Me either. Someone got to her." Griff said, reaching for one of Agnes's much cherished onion rings only to have his hand slapped.

"I don't really care what happened. She's taken a step in the right direction."

"Wow, you've changed," Griff said looking at her curiously. "That psych must be helping a lot."

"I think so in more ways than one."

"How so?"

Agnes stopped chewing and looked at the burger she was holding.

"I'm beginning to understand myself. Who I am. What I am."

"You're a wonderful person, Aggie. I know we were never right for each other but we had a lot of good times. Maybe if I had been a better husband—"

"That's behind us. It's who we are now that counts. Don't get me wrong. I have a lot of issues to work out. It's not going to be easy, but I'm getting there."

"That's great!" Griff took an enormous bite from his burger and leaned back.

"So how's Jeff?"

"What makes you think I would know how he is?"

Agnes smiled.

"I suspect you like him more than you're saying. How is he?"

Griff shook his head.

"He called me earlier today. The last victim was someone he knew. It really shook him up."

"That's awful! Is he okay?"

"He's a tough kid. Reminds me of you a bit, when you were young and less jaded."

Agnes snorted and quickly swallowed.

"We're nothing alike."

"I didn't say you were alike. I said he reminded me of you. You remember how your mom used to rag on you about your work? Women didn't belong in law enforcement. How many times did we have to listen to that at Sunday dinners? Well, Jeff's parents felt the same way about him, and here he is with all the enthusiasm of a bear in a honey hive. You used to be that way."

"I did once. I've grown a lot wiser," Agnes replied.

"Yeah, the world does that. Too bad. I think Jeff is going through one of those growing pains."

"Well, it looks like he's got you to help him out. Look, Matthew could use some help up at the cabin. Bring Jeff when you start the addition."

"That's an idea," he said slowly. "I'll check to see how he feels about it and let you know. Ya know, Aggie, you really have changed. I'm happy for you…and proud of you."

Agnes didn't know how to respond, so she didn't.

Chapter 37

Marcella wore her black wig to the police station. In a way she felt like she was entering the confessional. The officer at the front desk was cordial. He escorted her to a small room with a table and several chairs. It was empty.

"The detectives will be here shortly. Can I get you something to drink? Water or coffee?"

"No, thank you." Marcella knew that police used the drink thing to get DNA.

She expected to wait a long time having read that was another tactic police used to break suspects. When the door opened moments later she was surprised to see her attorney, Brian Lots, followed by two other men.

"Nice to see you, Marcella," Brian said.

"It's been awhile," she replied, shaking his hand and then turning to the other men.

"Ms. Salvatore, I'm Detective Jeff Roberts. This is Ranger Lou Chapman." Jeff pointed to the older man who quietly took a seat at the table across from the woman. "May I call you Marcy?" He asked as he pulled a chair out and made himself comfortable.

"My friends call me Marcella. We've only just met."

Jeff looked up from his file. The woman's voice was cold and impersonal, very much like her expression. The painted-on eyebrows were exactly like Madeline had described.

"I apologize, Ms. Salvatore. I hoped we could keep this as friendly as possible," Jeff said.

"I wish to remind everyone that my client is here voluntarily," Lots interrupted taking the seat next to his client.

"No problem, Mr. Lots. Would either of you like something to drink before we get started?"

"Your desk officer already asked me that. The answer was no then and now." Marcella looked at the Ranger beside the young detective. "Isn't Ranger Lovejoy going to be here? I've been avidly following her progress on the Rapture Killer. She's quite fascinating."

Lou's lips edged up into a half a smile.

"Why would you think this is about that?"

"What else is this about? I doubt if a Ft. Worth detective and a Texas Ranger would be working together on more than one case." Marcella smiled. "Of course I could be mistaken."

"You could be," Lou said. "But we're not here to waste your time or ours. We only have a few questions about a car Hector Torres loaned to you."

Marcella sat back.

"What about it?"

"We believe it was used in a crime." Jeff forced a smile on his face. "Before we begin, do you mind if we record this interview?"

"As long as I have access to the transcripts, we're agreeable," the attorney said.

"No problem." Jeff identified the date, time, and all the occupants in the room after switching on the recorder.

"Now, Ms. Salvatore, as I said earlier, Mr. Hector Torres loaned you a car recently. Is that correct?"

"Hector has lent me cars several times. What do you mean by recently?" Jeff told her the dates. "That's right."

"Did you loan the car to anyone else while it was in your possession? Or notice it was missing at any time?"

"One question at a time," the attorney warned.

"No and no," Marcella said.

"Would you mind telling me where you went in the car? I mean did you take it out of town at any time?"

"Detective…"

"Sorry, Counselor. Did you take the car out of town?"

"I drove to Odessa for a few days, but I'm sure you know that already, Detective Roberts. Hector knew where I was going."

"Excuse me," Lots interrupted. "Is my client a suspect in your case?"

"At this time we're only trying to get details about the vehicle, Mr. Lots. As we've said, we believe it was used during a crime around the time it was in Ms. Salvatore's possession. This meeting is to clarify that. If or when she becomes a suspect we'll make sure to read her her rights."

"Good! We understand each other then," Lots said. "Sorry, Marcella, go ahead."

"I suppose someone could have taken the car while I was asleep or involved with my clients."

"What kind of work do you do?"

"I market and maintain gym equipment. It's easy to lose track of time when I'm working."

"So you were in Odessa on business?" Jeff asked as he jotted down responses and additional questions in his notebook.

"I just said that," Marcella said slowly.

"So you did." *You're an arrogant bitch.* "Do you always use Mr. Torres's cars on your out-of-town business trips?" he continued, keeping a neutral tone.

Marcella looked at Brian. Hector had recommended him several months ago. She had used him to handle a few business transactions and found him very competent. Hector recommended only the best people.

"Move on, Detective," Lots advised.

"Certainly," Jeff answered, never taking his eyes off Marcella. "I was just curious."

Marcella licked her lips and sighed.

"I sometimes use my personal car when I'm close to home. Normally I use the company van if I'm transporting equipment or traveling long distances."

Jeff's ears perked up at the mention of a van.

"Company van? Your employer furnishes you with a van?"

"How many times am I going to have to repeat my answers?" Marcella asked, sarcastically. "Yes! They give me a van."

"Why didn't you drive the van to Odessa?"

"I didn't need it for this trip. No equipment to haul, and my car was in the shop."

"So you called Mr. Torres and asked for a loaner."

"Now you're getting it, Detective."

"I'm sorry if I'm irritating you, Ms. Salvatore. I know this can be tedious but I don't want to make any mistakes. You understand!"

"Oh, I understand perfectly," Marcella replied, crossing her arms and leaning back in the chair. "Let's simplify this a bit and save both of us some time. Hector is an old friend. Actually, more than a friend to be exact. We're to be engaged. I believe that provides me with privileges he wouldn't normally extend to others."

Jeff also sat back in his chair, assuming a more relaxed position. Scanning his notes he checked off several items before looking up.

"The loaner was for a few days. Can you account for all your time during that period?" He watched as Brian Lots leaned over and whispered into his client's ear. Marcella nodded and turned back to him.

"I would have to look at my appointment book. Naturally, I don't keep track of every minute of every day. A lot of time was spent at my motel in between appointments. I do like to sleep occasionally."

"Were you alone at your motel?"

"That's none of your business," Marcella replied coolly.

"Did you go anywhere, aside from your clients' place?" Jeff asked, sitting forward again and poising his pen to write.

"Again none of your business."

Lou cleared his throat.

"Ma'am, we need to know where the car was at all times. If it was taken by someone without your knowledge, it had to be when you were somewhere for several hours. That means your hotel, your client or perhaps a restaurant or club. Is there any possibility that you visited a club or bar that caters to your type?"

The corner of Jeff's mouth barely twitched as Marcella's face turned red.

"You're out of line, Ranger," Lots said. "One more stunt like that and we're leaving."

Marcella put her hand on her attorney's arm.

"Just a minute, Brian, I'd like to know what Ranger Chapman means by *my type*."

"I think you know, Ms. Salvatore. You said you were to be engaged with Mr. Torres but aren't you, in fact, a lesbian?"

Brian Lots jumped up from his chair and leaned across the table, making eye contact with the smug Ranger.

"I already warned you, Chapman. We're finished with this interview. Come on, Marc—"

"Ms. Salvatore," Jeff interrupted. "I apologize for Ranger Chapman's behavior. Please stay and answer a few more questions. If you want he can leave." Jeff glared at his companion.

"Detective Roberts," Marcella said, giving Chapman a dismissive look. "I'm not a stupid person. I know about the good-cop, bad-cop routine. I assume you're supposed to be the good cop so I'm willing to play this game a little longer if for no other reason than it amuses me. Sit down, Brian."

"Thank you," Jeff said, flipping to a new page in his notebook. "We would still like to know if you went out on the town while you were in Odessa."

"I'm not going to answer that," Marcella repeated and folded her hands, laying them in her lap.

"That does pose a problem for us then," Jeff said. "The vehicle was definitely used in the commission of a crime. The victim was a known lesbian. Friends at a club on the night of her disappearance said she left with a woman no one had seen before." Jeff placed the composite drawing that had been made from Madeline Owens's description. Then he placed three more drawings from other witnesses who were regulars at the bar and had seen the victim that night. "I'd say that you closely resemble this person, except for the hair. One clearly mentioned…" Jeff looked directly into Marcella's eyes, "…unusual eyebrows." He pulled another picture out of the file, a picture of Brat he had gotten from Telly. "Do you recognize this young woman? She was about to turn twenty-three. In a few months she was graduating from UTA with a bachelor's in English."

Marcella looked down at the photo of her last victim. Her mouth curled into a sneer.

"She was Godless!" Marcella spat out.

"Marcella," Brian warned, "that's enough! Don't say another word."

"Shut up, Brian! I don't take orders from you or anyone, only a higher power! You're a tedious little man who's starting to annoy me. If you can't be quiet, go on back to Hector. I don't need you here anymore!" Marcella knew the game was over. She was almost grateful in a strange way, but wasn't going to make it easy for the police. "You can't prove anything," she said to Roberts after the attorney left.

"Oh, I think I can, Ms. Salvatore, and because of that, I now have to make sure you're Mirandized."

"Don't be ridiculous. I know my rights so let's not play games any longer. You tell me what you think happened and I'll tell you if you're full of shit."

You're a tough bitch! Jeff thought. *I wish Agnes was here. She'd know how to handle you.*

"Okay, Ms. Salvatore. Here goes. This is what I think happened. You met Brat at The Fruit Jar for a date. Wanda Jenkins introduced you to her after you saw her in the gym. Telly, the bartender, talked with you. Both will testify you left with her. You were good at cleaning up after yourself with the other victims but you didn't have time to take care of Brat. Of course, there were other witnesses in the bar who are willing to pick you out of a lineup. Oh, and this woman as well." Jeff placed a photo of Madeline Owens on the table. "The one that got away. She gave us the best composite description of you and swears she can pick you out of any crowd if she ever saw you again. Considering the amount of time you two spent together in your car, she's going to be a very credible witness, don't you think?"

Marcella took a deep calming breath, still unwilling to give in until she got what she wanted.

"What I think is, it's time I talked with Agnes Kelly-Elliott."

Stunned, Detective Roberts and Ranger Chapman stared at their suspect in disbelief.

Chapter 38

"I want to talk to Agnes Kelly-Elliott."

Jeff's eyebrows shot up.

"She doesn't work for the department anymore."

Lou leaned forward. His eyes narrowed.

"Why on earth would you want to talk to her?"

Marcella met the Ranger's stare unflinchingly and somewhat arrogantly. A glint of madness seemed to appear, especially when her lips turned slightly upward at the corners.

"She's the only one who will understand." Marcella felt energized, and with it a sense of power. "What was the last count?"

"Excuse me?" Jeff asked, quite sure he had not heard correctly.

"The body count. Isn't that what you call it? How many souls do you think God has received thanks to your *Rapture Killer*? It's a simple question." Marcella wanted to know if the police numbers matched her own. She suspected they weren't even close.

Jeff mentally clicked off the information he had been given by Lovejoy and the other police departments around the state.

"Ms. Salvatore, before we continue I have to read you your rights. You have the—"

"I know my rights, Detective. I'll let you know when I want an attorney. I've been cooperative so far. Now it's your turn to answer my questions. How many?"

"You tell me," he replied, unwilling to give her an answer yet.

Marcella grimaced.

"I'm not sure that's in my best interests, but I'll make it easier for you…less than a dozen I imagine."

Jeff nodded his head slowly.

"What a shame! I'd have thought more…" Marcella's head tipped to the side. A thin smile pulled at her lips. "Considering how prolific this Rapture Killer was. Of course, you did say one got away, didn't you?"

"She was your first big mistake, Ms. Salvatore," Jeff said.

"My mistake?" Marcella's smile widened. "I haven't confessed to anything. Still, she is a fortunate young woman, isn't she? You didn't make her escape public. Why?"

"We thought you might try to come back for her."

Marcella looked pensively at her hands. Her fingers were casually interlocked and resting on her lap.

"Mm…you keep saying **you,** meaning me, of course, so I'll play your game. It's all really speculation, though, isn't it? A game, so to speak. Let's see…maybe she wasn't an intended victim. Maybe she was just a mistake. Anyway, when I asked about body count, your number seemed…well…*low.*" Jeff gave her a confused look. Marcella's fake eyebrows shot up in mock surprise. "I guess you all haven't done your homework."

"There're others?"

"Oh, Jeff…I *can* call you Jeff, can't I?" Marcella laughed. "You guys really are clueless aren't you? Skills need to be honed. One doesn't learn a trade overnight."

"So you admit—"

"I'm not admitting to anything, at least not to you. I said this was a game, all theoretical stuff. You think you have enough evidence to convict me? I seriously doubt it. A couple of composite drawings? How many women look like those images? I imagine my attorney could find a dozen in less than thirty minutes. Hell, half of Hector's female employees probably fit those sketches. As for the loaner car, lots of people have access to that vehicle. It's a fleet car. Hector knew where I was staying. Maybe he killed that woman and set me up. He travels a lot. Did you find any DNA or hair samples to compare with mine?" Marcella shook her head slowly. "I doubt it…other than in that one car. A good attorney will tear your evidence apart. A great one won't even let it go to trial. All an attorney needs is to create the benefit of the doubt."

Closing his notepad, Jeff slipped it into his jacket pocket.

"What kind of game are you playing, Ms. Salvatore?"

"The same one you're playing, Detective. You didn't bring me in here to simply discuss that car. I was your newest suspect. Well, I'm willing to give you what you want if I get what I want."

"Why would you do that?"

"For fun? Because I like seeing all of you squirm?" Marcella laughed at the stunned expressions on the two officers' faces. "Or maybe I'm tired. I suppose *if* I were the person you were looking for I could confess. That would make things too easy for you. Frankly, this isn't about you, is it? You're not the person I want to talk to."

"Why Detective Kelly-Elliott?"

"I have my reasons. It's her or no one." Marcella took a deep breath to settle her rapidly beating heart. She was taking a huge gamble. If the police refused to meet her demands she wasn't sure what she would do. They had enough probable cause to keep her locked up for seventy-two hours without charging her. Even Hector couldn't prevent that. If they decided to chance an arrest they could keep her longer, possibly weeks before an arraignment hearing and they probably did have enough circumstantial evidence to present a reasonable case.

"Not going to happen. She's no longer a cop," Jeff said, interrupting her thoughts.

"That's too bad. I guess we have nothing more to say to each other." Taking out her cell phone, she held it up. "Should I call my attorney back?"

Jeff looked at Lou who was looking at the mirrored-glass on one wall. A soft tap from the other side called a temporary halt to the interview. Marcella smiled. She had gotten someone's attention. She knew who was behind the mirror.

"I think Ranger Lovejoy wants in on this. She's on the other side of the glass, isn't she? Oh, and don't forget to switch off the recorder. I'm getting quite bored with all of this." Marcella fell silent.

"I'll be right back. Excuse us." Jeff motioned for Lou to follow him. Once outside the room he signaled to a female uniformed officer, throwing his thumb over his shoulder. "Watch her. No talking. If she wants to say something, listen." The officer nodded.

†

"This is the weirdest thing I've ever heard of," Lou said. "Does anyone even know where Elliott is?

"Who cares?" Cochetta asked. "She's not talking to her. This is police business." Cochetta turned toward the Assistant DA. "Right?"

Smith, the ADA, shook his head.

"I need to run this by my boss. This certainly is irregular but if Detective Kelly-Elliott can get a confession, it'll certainly make things easier." Smith took out his phone and dialed his office.

"This is ridiculous. I'm not letting—"

"Shut up, Lovejoy," Lou said. "I'm in charge now. That nut in there has just hinted there are more victims than we realized. We need to know who and where. I wonder why she wants to talk to Elliott," he added. Lou glanced sideways at Cochetta. "Any guesses?"

Cochetta shook her head. "She's crazy! That's explanation enough."

A few minutes later Assistant District Attorney Smith slid his phone into his pocket.

"The boss is on his way. He wants no one else talking to her until he gets here. He asked if we Mirandized her. I had to tell him no."

"We were just interviewing her, for Christ's sake," Lovejoy said. "Besides, she told us to forget it. She's the one who brought up the body count shit. It's all on the recorder."

"Well, if we can get her to sign a document saying she's waived representation, we should be okay. If she talks with Elliott I need to be present with one officer. Every second must be taped with no starting and stopping. One more important thing. No press…no leaks. I don't want another debacle like the last one. The city already has enough problems with your last mistake." He leveled his gaze at Cochetta. "Understood?"

"Perfectly!"

"Good, now all we need is Ms. Kelly-Elliott," Smith said, looking at Jeff who was talking animatedly into his phone.

Chapter 39

Griff was in the middle of lugging a box into the living room when his cell phone rang.

"Elliott," he said, balancing the box on his knee with one arm. "Yeah, I'm at her place now. Hold on!" Motioning for Agnes to come over, he held the phone out. "It's Jeff. He needs to speak to you."

"Hello?" She then listened as Jeff rattled off a long explanation about the department's dilemma. When he finished, she slumped against the wall and stared blankly at Griff.

"What is it?" he asked as he watched Agnes's features morph from confusion to shock.

"They think they have the Rapture Killer. She wants to talk to me. Why would she want to talk to me?" Agnes asked.

Griff took the phone from Agnes's hand and spoke into it.

"Jeff? What the hell is going on?" He listened intently as he watched Agnes processing the same information Jeff gave him. "She'll call you back. No, I don't know when." Shutting off the phone he looked worriedly at Agnes. "What do you want to do?"

"Certainly not that!"

"Then tell them to tell her to go to hell! You don't owe the department anything."

"I know but if they do have the killer, what choice do I have?" She said walking over to sit on the edge of the couch.

"Two choices, Aggie, go or don't go. They can do this without you."

"I know. If they have to turn her loose, she could kill more women before they have enough to charge her." Agnes stood and looked down at herself. She had on ripped cut-off denim shorts and a faded blue T-shirt. "I need to change."

Griff slammed the box he was holding onto the floor.

"Damn stubborn—"

"You want to come along?" Agnes asked as she went over to a stack of boxes and began digging through them for clothes.

"Why are you doing this, Aggie? What do you owe those assholes? Fucking Lovejoy and the rest can handle this."

"Griff, she says she'll confess, but only to me. Jeff said there are probably more victims. I couldn't live with myself if that were true and I did nothing. Maybe you should stay here and finish with the packing. It'll save me a lot of time." Agnes turned back to the box and pulled out a pair of jeans and a black T-shirt.

Griff huffed.

"You aren't going through this alone again. I'm going with you," Griff shouted after her and then mumbled. "Damn fool woman."

"I heard that!" Agnes yelled back.

Griff picked up his cell phone—one call to Jeff and one to Cindy Schultz.

Chapter 40

Cindy Schultz had an evening of surprises. She hadn't heard about Ranger Lovejoy stepping down the day before. Griff's call caught her off-guard. After listening to his agitated ramblings of what was happening, she agreed to meet them at the station.

The lobby was packed with people. Saturday evenings were always busy. The desk sergeant didn't even try to stop her as she walked past him and down the hallway toward the Homicide department. She searched for Agnes or Griff amongst the crowd in the office, but didn't see them. A tap on her shoulder startled her. Turning she saw Jeff standing behind her.

"Detective Roberts," she greeted curtly.

"Ms. Schultz, Griff called and said you would be here. I'm glad. What do you know about the situation?" Jeff clasped Cindy by the elbow, guiding her to a quiet corner.

"Not much. Mr. Elliott was extremely agitated. He said Agnes was coming here to talk to some whacko about the killings." Cindy glanced around.

"We have The Rapture Killer in Interview One," he said excitedly.

Cindy's eyes went wide.

"No shit?"

"No shit." Jeff smiled and then leaned forward to whisper, "She wants to confess, but will only talk to Agnes."

"Why Agnes?"

"That's what we'd all like to know. It's her or nothing."

"I don't like this," Cindy said. "Agnes isn't a detective anymore. What does the DA have to say?"

"He's the one who told us to call her."

Cindy shook her head.

"I want transcripts of whatever is said in that meeting."

"You know we can't—"

"Agnes is my client. You and the city falsely accused and arrested her. We have filed a civil suit. Agnes is under no obligation to cooperate with you. Either I get the transcripts or we're out of here the minute she arrives. Run it past the DA and let me know. I'll wait in here."

"Okay." Jeff fidgeted uncomfortably. Cindy gave him a curious look.

"Anything else, Detective Roberts?"

When Jeff blushed she frowned.

"Ms. Schultz, I know this isn't the time or place but…well…"

"Well, what?"

"Never mind. Maybe we can talk later."

"What is it, Detective?"

Turning an even brighter red, Jeff glanced around and then looked down at his shoes.

"Would…would you like to go to dinner with me sometime?"

"What? You're actually asking me out at a time like this?"

"I'm sorry. I don't know what I was thinking." Jeff rubbed his face with his palm. "This shit is really getting to me. Look…"

"You weren't thinking," Cindy replied. "And I don't date cops." Jeff looked crestfallen. "It's a policy I have."

"That's okay. It's actually probably a good one."

Cindy looked surprised.

"Really? You think so?"

"Yeah. We're not exactly the best catches. It's just, well, the first time we met, I felt a connection. Silly." Jeff shrugged. "Why the no cops rule?"

"Cops are arrogant asses, with infallibility complexes." Cindy rattled off several more reasons ending with, "They enjoy their power."

"Sounds like lawyers to me," Jeff replied with a mischievous smile. "You could set your policy aside once, you know. Test your theory. A dinner with me might prove you wrong." He tilted his head and smiled as sweetly as he could.

Cindy bit the inside of her cheek to keep from returning the smile. She looked away, trying to compose herself.

"You don't give up very easily, do you?"

Jeff grinned. "I'm a cop. Persistence is my middle name."

She shook her head.

"Call me tomorrow, persistence. I'll let you know then." Reaching in her pocket she pulled out her business card.

"At least it's not a no," he said, slipping the card inside his wallet.

When he heard his name called from across the room, Jeff looked up annoyed. Cochetta Lovejoy was walking toward them.

"Elliott's here. The desk sergeant just called…" Cochetta began and then stopped. "Ms. Schultz."

"Ranger Lovejoy," Cindy replied coldly.

"Why are you here?" Cochetta asked. She knew the attorney was gunning for her and going after the city of Ft. Worth for Agnes's arrest. "Smell blood in the water?"

"At least what I smell is real. Don't think for a moment you stepping down as lead investigator changes a thing. You fucked up, Ranger. I'm dragging you and everyone involved in her false arrest down."

"I was doing my job. Maybe I did make a mistake."

"Maybe?"

"Okay, I moved too quickly. Elliott…" Cochetta stopped. "Ms. Kelly-Elliott was a cop. She'd…"

"Don't even dare to finish that sentence, Ranger. Agnes's life is in shambles. She's lost her job, her family and most of her friends. That doesn't even come close to what happened to her in prison. How do you fix any of that?"

"I…I don't know. What can I do?"

"Make a public apology. The city will be more willing to settle her case if you admit to your mistake. At least it will save her the humiliation of having to relive everything at a trial. Think about it,"

Cindy said and walked away when she saw Agnes and Griff enter the room. Agnes looked confused. "Griff called me," Cindy explained coming to a stop in front of her client.

"I thought Cindy should know before you went through with this," Griff said.

Agnes nodded. "Thanks. I'm not feeling so sure I'm doing the right thing now."

"They can wait," Cindy said, looking over her shoulder at Cochetta and Jeff who were slowly making their way toward them. "Why did you think you should do this?"

"I can make a difference," Agnes said with more conviction than she felt.

"Can't we all," Cindy said cynically, putting on a fake smile for the Ranger and detective.

"Hey, Agnes," Jeff said with a nod.

"Hey." Agnes looked at Lovejoy. "Are you sure you have the right person this time?"

Cochetta took a deep breath.

"We're sure. Look, Agnes, I'm no longer in charge of the investigation. Ranger Chapman is running things. He's on a call right now so I've been asked to brief you on what the DA wants to do."

"Does your suspect have legal representation?" Agnes asked.

"Her attorney was here earlier, but she sent him packing. The DA prepared documents for her to sign. She's also agreed to have an officer in the room with you," Jeff said and noticed the glare Agnes gave Cochetta. "One of ours, Agnes. Mary Sutton will sit in."

Agnes visibly relaxed.

"Anything else I should know?"

"We have witness statements and composites you'll need to review, along with the case file. You don't have much time for that so I've written several questions I'd like you to ask," Cochetta said, handing the thick file to Agnes.

"I've run interviews before."

Cochetta sighed.

"Could we talk privately for a moment?"

"No way," Cindy cut in. "This is strictly about your suspect."

"Interview One, right?" Agnes asked.

"I'll be outside the door with Griff," Jeff said. "If you need anything, we'll be there for you."

"Damn straight," Griff agreed.

"Okay." Agnes took a deep breath.

"You don't have to do this, Agnes," Cindy said.

"I do. Let's go." She turned and headed down the hall, glancing quickly through the folder. Mary Sutton was resting against the wall outside the interview room.

"Did you draw the short straw, Mary?"

Mary Sutton smiled and stood to her full six-foot height. "Hell no, but no one wanted to say theirs was smaller."

Agnes liked Mary. She was a good cop, a good detective, and a good person.

"Have you had a chance to go over this?" Agnes held up the file.

"Jeff let me have a peek. I'm here strictly to keep things legal. It's your show," Mary said.

"Thanks. Give me another couple of minutes to check this out."

"Take all the time you want," Mary replied. "No one's going anywhere."

Agnes nodded as she flipped through the most recent entries. A lot of the information she was already familiar with because of the file Jeff had left with her. When she was done she made eye contact with the uniformed officer who was standing just outside the door.

"Open up," she said. Stepping inside she nodded to the officer on the other side of the room leaning against the wall. "Thank you, Sgt. Nevin, we've got it." Agnes waited until the woman left and then studied the suspect seated at the table. Mary sat down next to her. The mirrored wall was beside them giving the people on the other side a clear view of everyone in the room.

Marcella looked to be of average height, slender but fit. Her hair was stark black, obviously a wig and her eyes coffee brown. High cheekbones and full lips finished off a somewhat comical but attractive package. If it weren't for the painted on eyebrows… Agnes barely controlled a shake of her head.

"Ms. Salvatore, I'm Agnes Kelly-Elliott. Before we begin I have some documents that you agreed to sign." Agnes carefully spread the waivers out on the table. "Before you do that, though, I'm going to have Detective Sutton read you your rights."

"Sure, why not? We must keep things legal." She listened while Sutton read the list from a card she had pulled from her shirt pocket.

"…do you understand these rights as I've explained them to you?" Mary asked.

"Perfectly." Marcella accepted a pen from Mary and signed the paperwork.

"Do you wish to have an attorney present while being questioned in these matters?" Mary asked.

"No." Marcella looked at Agnes. "Kelly will do."

Agnes had been looking over the questions when Marcella said Kelly.

"Excuse me?"

Marcella smiled.

"You don't recognize me, do you?"

"We've met before?" Agnes tried to place the woman's face, but came up blank. Then Marcella reached up and pulled her wig off.

"Holy crap!" Mary said from beside her.

Marcella dipped her right index finger into her left eye. When she pulled her finger away a dark brown contact rested on her fingertip. Marcella repeated the action with her right eye. Agnes stared into blue-green eyes.

When Agnes gave her a blank look, Marcella shook her head.

"You still don't recognize me do you? Maybe it's the hair, or lack of, I should say. It used to be long." As recognition dawned in Agnes's eyes, Marcella smiled, smugly satisfied. "It's been awhile," she said.

Chapter 41

The observation room erupted in chaos.

"I fucking knew it!" Cochetta yelled triumphantly.

Cindy was shaking her head.

"No way. That's not possible."

Cochetta jabbed a finger toward the glass.

"Your client is part of this!"

Lou Chapman didn't know what to think anymore.

"Could we all settle down? We need to find out a little more before we rush off to crucify Elliott again."

"She doesn't leave this building," Cochetta ordered.

"Pipe down, Ranger." Cindy said annoyed. "I'd like to hear what Ms. Salvatore has to say."

†

Marcella's laughter had an almost a maniacal quality. Agnes excused herself from the table and left the room. Jeff and Griff both stared at her as she paced the hall. She didn't notice Rangers Lovejoy and Chapman joining the onlookers.

†

Agnes remembered Marcella. She had returned to Sophie's Choice after Cochise stormed out of her hotel room. Her libido was raging and the evening was still young. The bar was crowded. It was almost impossible to get the bartender's attention. Agnes was about to give up when an arm extended past her and knocked the bottom of a beer mug against the wood bar. The loud bang accomplished what Agnes's hand signals couldn't.

"It seems to get a little crowded in here after eleven, huh?" The woman who had pounded the bar commented from slightly behind her. The warmth of her closeness sent a pleasant shiver along Agnes's spine.

"It wasn't this busy earlier," Agnes replied.

"Yeah, I saw you then. Then you disappeared with someone. I take it things didn't work out so well."

Agnes shrugged, thanking the bartender for bringing her drink. Turning around she was pleasantly surprised to see a nice-looking woman in faded blue jeans and sleeveless white blouse. The exposed arms were well muscled.

"We don't like the same things. Are you a regular?" she asked, looking directly into blue-green eyes.

"Oh, no. Not me. I'm new at all this." The woman blushed and looked away. "But I'm learning quickly. You have to get the bartender's attention by pounding your mug."

"Better late than never." Agnes raised her glass in salute and downed her drink. "Would you care to sit with me…if we can find a table?" She received a hesitant nod that turned into a brilliant smile. "Great! What's your poison?" Agnes ordered drinks for both of them. They found a small table that was just emptying and sat down facing each other. Extending her hand Agnes introduced herself.

"I'm Kelly, and no, it's not my real first name." Her hand was taken in a firm shake.

"Marcy."

Agnes would never presume to ask for anything more in the way of introductions.

"So, not a regular. Are you from out-of-town?"

"Yes. You?"

"I'm definitely not from here. There's no way I would get away with this where I live," Agnes found herself confessing.

"I'm ashamed to say that I don't think I could get away with it either. My family is… conservative." Marcy played with a small golden crucifix at her neck.

Agnes nodded.

"Yeah, family. I know what you mean. Makes me wonder why we put up with them. You know what I mean?"

Marcy's head bobbed up and down enthusiastically.

"If mine could just see me for who I am. Sometimes they make me feel ugly…even dirty."

"You're definitely not ugly or dirty," Agnes said, reaching over to cover Marcy's hand with hers.

Marcy blushed and looked down into her drink.

"Thanks. You're not so bad yourself."

"Glad to hear that. Listen, I know I'm moving fast…and…well, if I offend you, I'm apologizing up front." Agnes took a deep breath. "You said you were new at this. Did you mean coming to a lesbian bar or were you looking for something more?"

"Both. But if you're asking me to leave with you, I'd like that."

Agnes set her glass on the table.

"You need to know what you're getting into, Marcy. I'm only after a one-night stand. I know that sounds crude but I want to be honest with you. And I like to be in control. Do you know how bondage works?"

Surprisingly Marcy nodded.

"That's the safe word-type thing. Restraints, power. All that stuff. I've always been curious about it."

Agnes smiled gently and moved her chair around next to Marcy's. She carefully explained what was involved. She could feel the heat rise off Marcy's body as she spoke. When she finished she sat back, waiting for a response.

Marcy's eyes darted to meet Agnes's even stare.

"Would you hurt me?"

Agnes shook her head.

"No, that's something entirely different. You might come away with a few fingernail scratches, but I assure you, I don't like inflicting pain. You're the one who really has the power, Marcy. A single word from you ends the whole thing." She watched as Marcy processed all the information given.

"I've never…"

"There's a first time for everything." Agnes rose and held her hand out for Marcy to take. "Come on. Let me be your teacher. If you don't like it, you'll know better the next time you meet someone who's into it."

Agnes led Marcy out of Sophie's Choice, but not before she caught a glimpse of Cochetta standing next to a woman at the far end of the bar.

Looks like I win, Agnes thought smugly.

†

Cochetta watched Agnes pace back and forth.

"You know her, don't you? She may not be your accomplice but you did something to make her this way."

"Fuck off, Lovejoy!"

"Not this time. Somehow you've created this monster," Cochetta accused, pointing her finger at Agnes. "You're responsible for what she is."

Agnes took a deep breath.

"No, I'm not, but you're right about me creating a monster. Make it two." She looked directly at Cochetta.

"Bullshit!" Griff said angrily, "You aren't responsible for other people's actions, Aggie. I don't know what happened between you guys but that nut in there was crazy before you ever met her. As for Lovejoy, she's just an arrogant fruitcake who needs to be taken down a few pegs."

Agnes looked at her ex and then Cochetta.

"Everything we do affects someone. Everything!"

†

190

Cochetta saw the anguish in Agnes's eyes. The realization that she, herself, had destroyed this woman's life was uncomfortable. For a moment, she closed her eyes, wondering if she could have done things differently. *Perhaps*, she thought. When she opened her eyes, Agnes was disappearing into the interview room. Cochetta met Griff's glare and Cindy Schultz's anger. "When will this be over?" Cochetta asked.

"For you, soon enough. Agnes will get you what you need to close the Rapture Killer case. You'll get the credit and the Rangers will have come to the public's rescue once again. For Agnes, never," Jeff said and walked back to stand with his shoulder next to the door. Griff followed without saying a word. Cindy disappeared into the observation room.

Cochetta felt very alone. Straightening her shoulders, she walked away, past the observation room and back toward the detectives' office.

✝

Inside the interview room, Agnes sat down and picked up the list of questions Lovejoy had given her. Much to Agnes's relief Marcella had put her wig back on.

"I'm sorry about that, Marcy…"

"Marcella. Do I call you Kelly or Agnes?"

"Agnes is fine." She sorted through the composites in front of her and found the one that resembled Marcella on the night she had met her. "This one, this is how I remember you. How did you know who I was? I mean that I was a police officer?"

Marcella took the paper from Agnes's hand.

"I saw your picture on the news, when they arrested you." Glancing at the composite, she nodded. "Yes, that was how I looked before I cut my hair. Wigs are a wonderful invention, don't you think? Then He changed my life."

"He?" Mary asked, and then glanced at Agnes apologetically.

Marcella's lips broke into a serene smile.

191

"Yes, God. He tells me when it's time for another soul to be saved."

"God? God talks to you?" Agnes asked, barely able to control her surprise.

"Sometimes. He showed me what I needed to do. At first it was only in my dreams," Marcella explained excitedly. Being able to share her experiences with someone other than a priest was lifting. "My mother thought I was imagining things. She accused me of being sacrilegious and made me go to confessional almost every day. I hated that! Hated her for doubting me. She doesn't doubt me anymore." The smile on Marcella's face raised the hairs on Agnes's neck.

"What do you mean? Why doesn't your mother doubt you now?"

"Mother was the first soul I saved."

"You killed your mother?"

For a moment Marcella looked confused and then laughed.

"Killed my mother? Of course not! I love my mother. She's a good Catholic. I simply made sure she stayed that way."

"I don't understand," Agnes said, shaking her head.

Marcella raised her right hand and drew an imaginary cross on her forehead with the tips of her fingers.

"She wears the cross permanently. What's that they say? Never leaves home without it; but I don't want to talk about her." Marcella leaned forward and stared into Agnes's eyes. "I knew this would end here with you, you know. He sent me a vision."

"So all of this began because of me?" Agnes asked, more than willing to leave the subject of Marcella's mom alone. Her insides churned. She wanted badly to throw up.

"Not exactly. You furnished the final piece to the puzzle. I knew God wanted me to save sinners. I just didn't know where to start or how. You made me feel comfortable. And the bondage. It was the perfect solution. Then when you came, you asked me for forgiveness. Don't you remember?" Marcella asked. "I didn't realize at the time the importance of forgiveness. Later I understood everything. He wanted me to save you but I didn't know that then.

The church says people like us are perversions. That one day we'll pay for our sins. I'm cursed with feelings for women. So are you, but…but I understand what has to be done to atone. He showed me how I could be saved…and others. You showed me how to gain their trust. You were my teacher."

Agnes's mind flashed backed to that evening. Marcella had been satisfyingly submissive, her orgasm powerful. When Agnes came she had whispered in Marcella's ear, 'Forgive me' seeking her own redemption.

"I remember," Agnes said and looked down, struggling to find her voice. "Can you tell me about your first victim?"

Marcella closed her eyes, remembering the young woman with the red-tipped black hair. She was pretty and delicate.

"She was from San Antonio. I was outfitting two new gyms there for a chain. It was a big contract." Marcella said proudly. "I rented one of those extended-stay motel rooms since I was going to be there for a couple of weeks."

"Are you certain you don't want a lawyer, Marcella?" Mary interrupted.

"Why? God is here with me. I don't need anyone else." Marcella smiled at Mary and then turned her attention back to Agnes. "She was so pretty. Worth saving."

"How did you kill her?"

"I really wasn't sure I could do it, especially after I came. It felt wonderful, but wrong. You understand, don't you, Agnes? That moment of total bliss and despair?" Agnes understood all too well, but remained silent. "I was sickened that I could find such pleasure in perversion. When I didn't release her immediately, she panicked. I guess the cuffs were too tight. They weren't padded like yours. The skin around her wrists and ankles ripped a little bit. Then I saw the blood. It was a sign. Jesus bled from the crown of thorns. These were like small crowns…the way they circled her wrists," Marcella reflected. "I smothered her with a pillow. It took longer than I thought. She wouldn't lie still. It looks so easy in the movies, but it actually takes several minutes and a lot of force."

Agnes swallowed and checked off the confirming information on the list.

"Why do you place them out in the open?"

"They need to see Christ when he comes for them."

"From the east?"

"Of course!" Marcella said, clapping her hands together. "You do understand. Pinning her eyes open was an afterthought. I thought that was pretty brilliant. I had to use some staples that I bent open. It was messy."

"And after that?"

"Oh, I bought straight pins. They worked perfectly. It was wonderful knowing they could see me and His arrival."

And so it went for several hours. Agnes asking questions, Marcella answering them. They finally came to the victim that was killed while Agnes was in jail.

"You changed. Escalated the…" Agnes wasn't quite sure how to describe the mutilations.

"You can say it. I had to show God I was the one doing all the work. They gave you the credit. That wasn't right," Marcella said angrily. "I sent those women to Him. He said I wasn't doing enough. Sent me a sign. It was in a movie. The killer hacked at his victim with a chainsaw. I thought about that, but the noise would be pretty loud, not to mention awkward. Then I saw a commercial advertising these special carving knives. They never get dull and they slice meat like butter." Marcella shivered in her seat. "Of course, I know how to keep a knife sharp but a craftsman has to have good tools. I didn't realize there would be so much blood. It took me a long time to clean up. I got better with practice, though."

Agnes read some field notes in the file.

"The police were impressed that you didn't leave any evidence about you at the scene."

"Really? Was Ranger Lovejoy there?"

Agnes scanned through the Ranger's reports.

"Yes. She states it was the most horrific site she had ever seen." She looked up at Marcella for a reaction and saw a pleased smile on the woman's face. "And thought I had a partner. She believed you were my protégé. Does that bother you?"

"Of course it does. Why should you get credit for my work? Saving souls is exhilarating, the begging for forgiveness, the blood…" Marcella's eyes closed remembering the warm fluid smeared across her skin.

"The blood," Agnes repeated. "Where did you learn how to clean up the victims so well? I don't think a forensics expert could sterilize a body like you did."

"Oh, don't worry, Agnes. You didn't have anything to do with that. I did my research. Did you know you can learn a lot of things watching police shows. Of course, most of the stuff you see is crap but not everything. And the Internet, it's an amazing source for information."

Agnes flipped to the picture of the body that had literally been partially de-fleshed.

"This woman. Was she alive when you did this?" Agnes asked, finding it more difficult to keep her anger in check.

"All of them were. Well, except one. I killed her too soon but God understood. The others needed to repent."

Agnes felt her stomach churning.

"Were they conscious?"

Marcella looked at Agnes like she was a bit crazy.

"That's a dumb question. They can't ask for forgiveness if they're unconscious."

"I need a break," Mary said quietly and quickly left the room.

Agnes wished she could just get up and leave, but Marcella was being so cooperative she didn't want to break the momentum. She could not imagine how the woman across from her had evolved into the unfeeling killing machine that she had become.

"Would you like a break? Can we get you something to eat or drink?"

"I knew you would be kind to me. You told me you would never hurt me," Marcella said with a look of trust and adoration.

"I'm glad I can help you through this, Marcella," Agnes lied. "And that you decided to end all of this."

Marcella reached across the table and placed her hand on Agnes's arm.

"Do you really think it's over? Is God satisfied with my sacrifices?"

Looking at the hand, Agnes chose her words carefully.

"I don't presume to know what God wants of us, Marcella, but if I were to guess, I'd say He was." Her answer seemed to satisfy Marcella. Agnes closed the folder, leaving the list of questions sticking out to mark her place. "The police will be in shortly to formally charge you. Are you ready for that?"

"Will you be back?" Marcella asked, showing the first hint of fear.

Agnes nodded.

"Yes, after a short break," she said softly, suddenly feeling sad for Marcella. The woman was horribly deranged. *What happened that made you this way?*

Jeff entered the room with two female uniformed officers. Agnes stood and stretched her back, giving him a grateful look.

"She's ready to be charged." Jeff nodded and then turned his attention to Marcella. He read off the charges. "Please make sure she gets something to eat before we begin again." She caught Marcella's attention with a gentle hand to her shoulder. "Do you want me to call anyone for you?"

"They won't come," Marcella said sadly. "I only have God, Jesus and you with me now. Mom will never understand me like you do."

Agnes watched as Marcella was led from the room. She didn't resist as she was steered down the long hallway.

Chapter 42

Agnes wanted to curl up in a ball and disappear. Outside of the police station the night was clear, the air heavy with a cold humidity. There were fewer stars visible in the city than at her cabin. She had grown accustomed to viewing the thousands through the canopy of leaves and branches. Agnes stood transfixed for a long time before a voice brought her back to reality.

"You did a great job in there. The ADA is happy," Jeff said from beside her.

Agnes hadn't even heard his approach.

"Business as usual." She smiled crookedly as she glanced at her ex-partner. "How are you holding up?"

Jeff pointed at himself.

"Me? How am I holding up? For Christ's sake, you're the one in there. How are you holding up?"

Agnes looked up at the stars once again.

"I'm the ice queen, remember." Several of her former colleagues had given her that name over the years. She was known for her cool exterior in the face of chaos.

"You're full of crap!" Jeff sighed and tilted his head back to take in the night sky. "None of this is your fault, Agnes."

Agnes blinked at the stars.

"I'll be sure to add that to my daily mantra."

The station door behind them opened. Mary Sutton poked her head out.

"We're ready to go again."

Agnes turned enough to nod at Mary.

"Thanks, I'll be right there." She looked at Jeff. "Ready to go?"

"With you, anywhere, anytime."

"Careful with your words, Jeff Roberts. They could come back to haunt you," Agnes said, turning to head inside.

Jeff beat her to the door.

"I've learned a great deal from you, Agnes. One of the first things you told me was to always say what I meant clearly. Your exact words were 'confusion can be an investigator's worst enemy. Ideas and thoughts must be presented in a precise and orderly manner so that all involved can participate in the discovery of facts.'"

Agnes paused.

"I said that?"

"The very first day I rode with you."

"And you memorized it?" Agnes asked in disbelief.

"Wrote it down so I could. You never noticed me scribbling the whole time you were talking?"

"I just thought you were one of those list makers." Agnes grinned and bumped her shoulder against his. "Come on. Let's see if we can wrap this up." They walked together back to the interview room. "Did Lovejoy enjoy the show?"

"She left. Someone saw her make three phone calls and hand a note to Chapman. After that…poof…gone," Jeff said as he looked down the hall at Cindy approaching. He couldn't help the smile that brightened his tired features.

Agnes looked between her friend and her lawyer.

"No cops, huh?" she asked Cindy.

Cindy smiled.

"I haven't agreed to anything."

"Yet. You two will either last forever or it won't go beyond the first date. I'm going to hope for the first." She then looked at Cindy. "What's up with Lovejoy?"

Cindy held up a tri-folded piece of paper.

"Resigned." She let Jeff take the paper from her hand. "She's given me a date and time for a deposition. If she follows through with the arrangement your case will be settled in one easy swoop.

After this bullshit, the price is going up." Cindy waved her hand toward the interview room.

Agnes thought she would be overjoyed to hear that Cochetta Lovejoy had resigned, but it only made her feel even more despair.

"I thought I would feel differently."

"Don't worry about her. She'll come out on top. She screwed you but I hear she's damn good at her job. I imagine she'll reconsider once she comes to her senses. Lovejoy likes Lovejoy too much to give up being a Ranger. She may be an ass but she's one of their shining stars…as long as it isn't personal. Her mistake was not recusing herself from this case the moment she saw you."

"What about the note?"

Cindy smiled.

"A souvenir. Whether she actually does or not, we at least have this. So, are you going back inside?"

"Yeah. We've got more victims to work through. The more details she's willing to give the stronger the case. There are also other victims out there we haven't found. Maybe we will after I'm done." Agnes looked at her watch, "I don't think I'll be much longer. I'm exhausted. Marcella probably is too."

"You can take the girl out of the cop shop, but you sure can't take the cop out of the girl," Cindy remarked. "They're lucky you're a good cop, Agnes."

"Was! It's all I ever wanted to do," Agnes said. "Maybe one day I'll do it again."

"I'll be first in line to ride with you, Agnes." Jeff held his hand out to her.

Agnes reached out and gave it a firm shake.

"I'll be the lucky one if we ride together again." She let go and entered the interview room. Mary was already seated. Marcella was sipping a soda. "How do you feel?" she asked as she sat down and once again opened the folder in front of her.

"Relieved," Marcella said with a weary smile. "Like an enormous burden has been lifted from my shoulders. You ever get that feeling?"

"Sometimes. Are you tired? We can stop for the night and pick back up tomorrow." Agnes was concerned they might be pushing the limits.

"No, I'm fine," Marcella assured her. "What was the name of the one who got away?"

Agnes didn't know that one had gotten away and had to look through the file.

"Madeline."

"I wasn't going to hurt her," Marcella said. "She was just a hitchhiker and straight. Said she had a boyfriend in the hospital. I hope he's okay. If it hadn't been for that flat, she'd have never seen what was in the trunk."

Agnes sat back.

"What happened with the last one? You came close to getting caught at the scene, right?" She remembered the details Griff had been able to give her.

"I...I don't know what happened."

Marcella looked remorseful causing Agnes to lean forward and rest her elbows on the table, her fingers loosely interlocked.

"Tell me about her. Everyone that saw you together thought you looked like a good match."

"We could have been. I wasn't going to kill her, you know. All she had to do was confess her sins." Marcella scooted forward and mirrored Agnes's pose. "The others, they were different...already hardened from their life of perversion...but Brat...she was sweet, innocent. I liked her," she said, looking away for a moment then back at Agnes. "She should have known who I was." Marcella reached out and moved the composite drawings on the tabletop around until she found the one she wanted. "This was pinned up behind the bar at the Fruit Jar. I know Brat and Telly must have seen it a dozen times. If either one of them had recognized me, Brat would still be alive."

"You're obviously pretty good at disguises, Marcella. I didn't recognize you at first."

Marcella blushed at the praise.

"I had to be."

"So, you say you weren't going to kill her. What changed your mind?"

"She was a nonbeliever."

"She was an atheist?"

"Yes," Marcella said sadly. "I tried to get her to accept Christ in her heart, but she refused. When she finally found the way, it was too late. She begged me to tell her what to say, but I couldn't. It had to come from her. Eventually she figured it out. Poor Brat! She was bleeding so badly I couldn't save her." Marcella's hands began to shake on the tabletop. "I ended it as quickly as I could. I hope she truly found God and wasn't just lying to stop me. She was a good kid."

"And what about you…your soul?"

Marcella looked down at her shaking hands and balled them into fists.

"I…I don't know. You see, the priests stopped giving me penance. They said I should go to the police. I prayed and prayed."

"So you knew you were doing wrong and wanted to stop?"

"I wanted direction. I sought guidance through prayer. I begged for a sign. Then it came to me." Marcella brightened some. "I knew what I had to do. My penance was to save these women before they went too far. That's why they had to be young. They still had a chance if they found God and repented."

"But the last one was different. You said you didn't want to kill her." Agnes pushed trying to understand.

"Brat! We could have been friends. If only she had accepted God sooner. All she had to do was ask His forgiveness." Marcella's hands slapped the tabletop as her anger flared. "She was a fool! Why didn't she see?" Marcella pounded the table. "I tried! I really tried!"

Agnes closed the file in front of her. She was sickened by what she had heard.

"We're finished now, Marcella. I won't be able to come back to talk to you. Detective Roberts will be taking over."

"Please don't go!" Marcella cried out, looking around her in panic. "You're the only one that understands. They don't know what it's like," she whispered, pointing toward the mirror.

"I'm not a cop anymore. There's nothing I can do."

Mary, who been sitting quietly next to Agnes, reached across the table and took one of Marcella's shaking hands in her own.

"I'll be here. I may not understand completely, but I won't leave you to deal with them alone."

Marcella looked at the tall woman with blue eyes and a kind smile. She then looked back at Agnes.

"She'll make sure you're okay. Mary can do things I can't. You understand?" Agnes asked, wanting some assurance from Marcella that she would at least try to keep the momentum going with the investigation. "There are consequences for what you've done, Marcella, consequences that you have to deal with. This is a matter for mortals now. You render unto Caesar what is Caesar's. That means us. You must tell us everything. If there are more women we don't know about, tell Mary or Detective Roberts. Help them give these women's bodies back to their families for proper burials. Put their bodies to rest so they can complete their journey. Will you do that?"

Marcella nodded.

"I'll tell them. I just want all of this over now…my life to be over."

Something in Marcella's tone bothered Agnes.

"You're not thinking of hurting yourself, are you? God forgives many things but not that," Agnes said with a stern gaze. "You need to answer for what you've done. That will be your real penance."

"Suicide is a sin, Agnes." Marcella straightened angrily. "My work was God's work."

"And so is this. We are all doing His work, now." Agnes took a big breath and exhaled slowly. "I'm just making sure you don't do something you'll regret. You've come so far today."

Marcella looked contrite.

"I wouldn't do that."

"Good." Agnes stood and the interview room door opened. Marcella was re-cuffed and taken away. Agnes handed the file back to Jeff. "Where's Griff?"

"Right here," Griff's rough voice answered from the doorway.

"Take me home, please."

✝

Griff knew instinctively that Agnes meant the cabin and not the house in the city. The drive was quiet and seemed to pass quickly. He crossed over the Red River just as the silver and red of the impending sunrise pushed away the blackness of the night. Agnes spent most of the trip staring out her window into the cold darkness. Griff pulled up the gravel road and stopped with Agnes's car door closest to the steps. They silently entered the unlit cabin.

"Do you want the bed?" Agnes asked.

Griff stared at her.

"With you in it? And I don't mean that like it sounds."

"No, I think I need to be alone. Thanks though." Agnes scrubbed at her face with the palm of one hand.

"Then I'll take the couch." Griff helped himself to the bathroom and then promptly passed out on the sofa.

Agnes changed into a warm pair of pajamas and stretched out on the bed. The soft goose down mattress cradled her sore and tired body. Minutes later she was sound asleep.

Chapter 43

A week later Cochetta gave her deposition to Cindy. Once it was typed and signed, Cindy made a list of everyone to be named in the lawsuit. Several public officials working for the city of Ft. Worth and the State of Texas were notified of her intent and requested a meeting with all of them prior to filing the paperwork, an unusual move. Within three days she had arranged a private meeting with almost everyone involved in the suit.

✝

Cindy circled the table placing a file folder in front of each person present. Once everyone had their copy, she returned to the head of the table and sat down. Leaning forward on her elbows she coldly eyed each one individually, making sure everyone understood **whom** they were dealing with. Four of the most powerful people in Texas were gathered in the conference room she had rented at The Omni Hotel.

Neutral territory! She had referred to it in her correspondence. Attorneys were welcome to come to the meeting but she encouraged everyone to attend the gathering alone. The information she was going to present might be better reviewed in privacy with what was going to be discussed.

✝

"First, ladies and gentlemen, I'd like to thank you for voluntarily coming here on such short notice. I know you have busy

204

schedules. I believe you know each other, except for Ms. O'Malley. At the moment she's here as an observer only," Cindy began.

"What's this about?" the mayor demanded. "I have several conferences scheduled later today."

"I'm sure you'll make them, Mayor. If not, it'll be because you decided this meeting was more important. Can I get anyone something to drink? You, Judge Elroy? Warden Labronin?" Swinging her head to the left she looked expectantly at the other members. "No? Well, let me know if you get thirsty. There's a lot of dry paperwork we'll be reviewing."

"Ms. Schultz, I don't understand the purpose of this meeting. I believe I'm not speaking out of turn by guessing that everyone in this room, excluding you and Ms. O'Malley, is about to be served papers for what happened to Detective Elliott. What happened to her was horrible but it didn't have anything to do with my department."

"On the contraire, Warden Labronin, if you open the portfolio in front of you, you'll notice several photos of wounds my client suffered while in your care. There are also statements from some prisoners and guards. Unfortunately no one was able to take pictures of the bruises from her beatings or the rape."

"I don't know anything about a rape," Labronin said, cutting Cindy off.

"You should have, Warden. That's part of your job. Now as I was saying, the photos are from the infirmary. The nursing staff is required to take pictures as documentation of all injuries requiring medical treatment. A policy you yourself set so the state and county would have another way to identify criminals by scars and to prevent lawsuits. Ironic, isn't it. You realize, of course, that these records will have to be destroyed once we settle our claim. The state has no right to these shots since my client was held illegally."

"We can't be blamed for her incarceration. It was ordered by Judge Elroy."

"True, and we'll be getting to her shortly. For now, though, I'm happy to address yours. Please look at the photos, Warden, and then the documents. None of them speak very highly of you."

"It's not my job to make guards or prisoners happy. I run a very tight ship."

"Yes, you do. So tight, in fact, that only privileged guards and prisoners get special treatment. Let's take for instance three female enforcers you've continually given privileges to. There's Karen "Big Tits" Riley…that's the picture labeled five, Sylvia "SJ" Jones, the scraggly haired blond, and Dixie "Dimples" Compton. These three women raped my client. They were also involved in an assault that sent her to the infirmary. The depositions in front of you state they are part of an elite enforcement squad, created by you, Warden Labronin. Their job is to keep the female prisoners in check, have them satisfy a few guards and get rewarded with a bit of coke and marijuana. And by coke I don't mean the soft drink." Cindy stared at the warden waiting for him to respond. When he didn't Cindy laughed. "Nothing to say? Too bad! I was hoping you would at least pretend to be innocent. I'd have loved to bring in a few witnesses. Oh well, maybe another time."

Walking to stand by the mayor, she flipped open the file in front of him.

"Now, Mayor Reyes, you are in a much better position than Mr. Labronin. You simply accommodated Ranger Lovejoy by putting pressure on Chief Chilton to expedite my client's arrest to minimize the political fallout for the city. I have statements from two anonymous sources that you told the chief to do whatever was necessary to make her go away. I believe your exact words were 'One bitch cop's ass isn't worth worrying about if it keeps the press off my back.' At the moment you're not the most popular politician so if I release this information to the public that 'bitch cop' is going to be humping your ass all the way to the bank…and your career will be over. The public may not always be on the side of the police, but they like political snakes even less."

Mayor Reyes opened his mouth to say something and then snapped it shut.

"My, my. When did you become a man of few words?"

Cindy moved to stand next to the final invited *guest*.

"Judge Elroy, you are the easiest to deal with. Judicial misconduct will definitely put an end to your career. I don't know what Ranger Lovejoy has on you but she used you to keep my client locked up without due process. She was conveniently denied counsel for weeks and her arraignment continually postponed. This makes you an accessory to assault and rape."

Judge Elroy pushed her chair away from the table and stood up. She was an impeccably dressed woman with gray hair pulled back into a bun. Although five three and slightly plump, she was still an imposing figure. Tugging her jacket down, she nonchalantly brushed a gray hair off her left breast pocket.

"That's absurd, young woman! You have nothing on me," she said coolly. "I've been a circuit judge for over fifteen years. I doubt if anyone of importance is going to believe anything you have to say. Now if you'll excuse me, I'll be going." Grabbing her handbag she headed for the door.

"I'd stick around, Your Honor," Ms. O'Malley said, quietly opening the folder in front of her. It was thicker than the others. As she shuffled through the paperwork she pulled out several documents and scanned them quickly.

"And exactly what is your role in all of this, Ms. O'Malley?" Judge Elroy asked. "Ms. Schultz conveniently neglected to tell us that."

"Like she said, I'm an observer, nothing more…but I've been given unlimited authority to pursue this matter further if this meeting proves to be nonproductive."

"Authority by whom?" Elroy demanded.

Ms. O'Malley sat back in her chair and looked around the table. Her dark brown eyes dared anyone to challenge her.

"By the governor, Mrs. Elroy."

"The…the governor?" Warden Labronin squeaked.

"Yes. You see, the governor isn't much different from you, Mayor. He enjoys the privileges of his position and would hate it if something damaged his political career. This type of publicity would create a lot of ammunition for his opponents so he'd like this to go away, quickly. Now, Ms. Schultz is going to present all of you with another proposition since you refused her first. If you're smart you'll take it. If not, I will open an investigation that will expose every detail of your sordid little lives and it won't stop there. Every family member, every friend, every work associate, past and present will come under my scrutiny. There won't be a minute of your life that will escape my aides or me. By the time I've finished with you, your careers will be over and all of you will know what it's like to be on the other side of those bars. The governor will be the hero of the day for exposing corruption at the highest levels and guaranteed another term." Standing she gathered up the folder and slowly pushed her chair against the table.

Cindy walked around the table handing everyone an envelope.

"And just where are we supposed to come up with all this money?" Warden Labronin asked, staring angrily at the settlement sum that was being demanded. "The insurance companies make the final decision in these matters."

"Not to mention there are several attorneys already involved. They're going to want an explanation and their money."

"That's not my, nor my client's, problem," Cindy said. "My suggestion is for each of you to fill the kitty with personal funds. Between the four of you, you've more than enough assets to meet our demands. Simply put, you pay and there's no lawsuit, no insurance or attorney involvement. All of this quietly goes away."

"How can we be guaranteed this?" the warden asked.

"Let's just say the files will disappear," Ms. O'Malley answered. "Don't get me wrong. Nothing is going to be destroyed. We're not that stupid. If the settlement is paid by private funds, the governor stays out of it. Of course there are a few more conditions he expects. Over the next few months, each of you is going to retire. Not all at once. That would seem strange and arouse suspicion. You're first, Warden Labronin. Before you do, make sure you reassign the correctional officers that were involved in *protecting* Ms. Kelly-Elliott to a maximum security men's prison…the general population. That should keep them sweating every day of their miserable lives. How the rest of you go, you work out." Turning to Cindy she cocked an eyebrow and smiled. "I believe you'll find your guests very open to your offer, Ms. Schultz. The governor is very appreciative that you have kept your demands so reasonable considering what your client was put through. I'm sorry I can't stay longer but I have to update him on this situation. Thank you for giving him this opportunity to assist you."

"My pleasure," Cindy said. After Ms. O'Malley left, she reached into her briefcase and pulled out a large envelope. Placing it on the table, she walked to the door. "I'm going to assume you're all in agreement with what's been proposed. The bank account information is in each one of your files as well as some documents to sign. Have a good day, boys and…girl."

✝

When Cindy called Agnes to tell her about the settlement, Agnes was overwhelmed with relief, not to mention stunned at the enormous sum of money she was going to receive. Per the agreement, the case was sealed by the governor. All Agnes was told was that no public funds were being used and those who colluded to have her charged and illegally detained were bearing the brunt of the settlement both financially and personally.

Marcella was arraigned six days after her confessions. She admitted to the twelve murders plus five more and was sentenced to multiple life terms due to a diminished capacity defense. Hector Torres had hired the best lawyers in the state. Many believed the sentence would eventually get overturned and Marcella would end up in an institution. Either way, she would never be released.

Epilogue

Instead of having Matthew, Jeff and Griff put on the addition Agnes hired a contractor to do the job. Her son and ex were frequent visitors, bringing whatever news from the city that seemed important. Her daughter had yet to contact her, and her parents had officially written her out of their lives. They had sent a courier with the letter. Agnes had broken several more dishes and then for some quirky reason sent the pieces back with the courier to her parents with a note that simply said 'broken lives.'

Summer was pushing spring away. The sky was a deeper blue and the air heavier. Agnes welcomed the change. Matt and Griff were coming later in the day.

It was a few minutes past six a.m. The sun was just painting the river with golden red rays. Standing next to the water, Agnes was enjoying the view when she heard someone come up behind her. Before she could turn she felt the muzzle of a gun against the back of her neck.

"Don't move!" Cochetta's voice was hard. "Are you armed?"

Agnes nodded her head slowly, motioning toward her jacket pocket.

Cochetta's free hand came around her, pulling her back into her. Cochetta then used her free hand to search for the small caliber handgun Agnes kept with her. Agnes's eyes closed as she heard it hit the riverbank.

"Not much of a weapon," Cochetta said. "That wouldn't stop a bear."

"It was never intended for a bear," Agnes said, hating that she couldn't control her trembling.

"What are you afraid of, Agnes? I'm not going to hurt you." The barrel of the gun left her head and the heat of Cochetta Lovejoy's body left her back. She spun around to face Cochetta. The Ranger had already holstered her gun. "I would never hurt you. Not again." Cochetta held her empty hands out at her sides. "But I couldn't count on you not to do the same after my last visit."

Cochetta never saw the slap coming. One minute she was standing within a foot of Agnes. The next she was backing away, her hand pressed against her stinging cheek.

"What the hell is wrong with you?" Agnes asked, her eyes blazing with rage. "I told you never to come here again!"

"This," Cochetta said, holding out Agnes's rosary, "I wanted to give this back to you."

"Bullshit! You could have mailed it." Agnes grabbed the rosary, jamming it in her pocket. "You've delivered it. Now leave!"

"Listen, Agnes, I really came to ask if you could…well, forgive me? I made a mistake but things turned out. We got the killer."

Agnes looked at the Ranger dumbfounded.

Did the woman really think… Taking a step toward her, she was pleased to see Cochetta back up.

"Turned out?" she asked, barely able to control the rage welling up inside of her.

"Umm, yeah. I mean about the killer. And you don't have to worry about your future now. The settlement…"

The second slap was harder than the first.

"Goddamn it!" Cochetta yelled, moving further away from Agnes.

"Settlement! You think everything's okay between us because of a fucking settlement?" All the force of Agnes's fury was being unleashed. "I've lost my family, my friends, and my job. What have you lost? Nothing! You're still wearing your gun so it looks like your resignation was a farce. What happened, Lovejoy? Did you get cold feet thinking about no longer being able to push people around? Or were you just too much of a coward?"

"I thought…"

"Thought what? You don't think at all. You're an arrogant, self-centered bitch who will do anything to prove yourself right no matter who gets hurt. You think because you have a badge you have the right to walk over anyone in your way. The fact that you're here proves it. I told you to stay off my property. You ignored that like you ignore anything else that doesn't suit you."

When Agnes took another step forward, Cochetta found herself backed to the edge of the river.

"Agnes, I came here asking to be forgiven, not to bother you," Cochetta said.

"You don't bother me," Agnes hissed. "You aren't important enough to bother me. As for my forgiveness…fuck you, Cochetta! And get the hell off my property!"

Spinning around Agnes marched off. The further she distanced herself from the stunned Ranger the better she began to feel. Things were definitely looking up. Agnes examined her right hand and smiled.

Damn that felt good!

About the Authors

A.C. Henley

A. C. Henley was born into a large family with varied belief systems and was the middle child of seven. Her parents were strong Catholics, yet her mother was also part Apache and those traditions were honored as well. Although A.C. came from mixed traditions, she was strong-willed as a young adult and began her intensive practice of self-inquiry then. This attribute appeared strongly in her writing and continued in her everyday life, as she became a strong woman who lived as a peaceful warrior in the modern world.

Although A. C. is no longer with us, her written words are still available. To contact A.C.'s partner Sherry, email her at barkerss1@att.net

Fran Heckrotte

Fran Heckrotte is the 2011 winner of the Alice B. Medal Award (http://www.alicebawards.org) and lives in the Sunny South with her husband, two dogs, Sophie and Skipper, koi, several goldfish and a yard full of chickens, moles and occasional snakes.

A few of her life experiences include living in Alaska for three years, gold panning, bull riding, scuba diving, flying, training gaited horses, and motorcycling. After spending five years in law enforcement, she switched to construction and eventually real estate. She now owns a small property management company.

Her hobbies include water gardening, landscaping, photography, hiking and skiing in Montreal when time allows. She credits her best friend for encouraging her writing. Fran loves interacting with readers and authors. You can find out more about work at her www.novelideaspublishing.com.

*

'55 Ford
Erin O'Reilly

Andrea McBride, the author of four books, wants to find someone to restore an old '55 Ford truck that she inherited in a real estate purchase. She will only settle for the best and finds RJ Whittaker who many proclaim to be the best restorer among millions.

*

**An Affair of Love
S. Anne Gardner**

From a dark past, a forbidden love, a secret comes. Among the confusion and the chaos of an unwanted reality, two women find something they neither want nor can deny.

*

**Desert Heat
Dannie Marsden**

For Luce Diamond, an undercover policewoman, her life is in shambles. Her longtime lover left her and an automobile accident that resulted in a child's death haunts her.

*

**Taming the Wolff
Del Robertson**

ONLY ONE WOMAN...
HAS THE POWER...
TO TAME THE WOLFF...

*

**Private Dancer
TJ Vertigo**

Reece Corbett grew up on the mean streets on New York City, abused, used and in trouble with the law.
Faith Ashford grew up wealthy, with all the creature comforts that money provides. When they meet fireworks begin.

*

Miriam and Esther
Sherry Barker

Miriam thought her life would play out in the bustling metropolis of Dallas, but after a life-changing accident, she moves to the small town of Cool Lake, Texas to get her head on straight and regain her senses.

*

McKee
A.C. Henley

Private Investigator Quinlan McKee has returned to Los Angeles after a three-year absence, only to find herself embroiled in a world of child slavery and police corruption.

*

Nocturnes
JD Glass

From acclaimed author, JD Glass, and featuring some of her most loved characters. Nocturnes is a collection of events and adventures, from the sensual dreamscape of the deepest love, to the brooding intensity of desire.

*

Miss-Match
AC Henley & Erica Lawson

Clancy Fitzgerald is twenty-nine, single, and a virgin. According to her aunt, she is as good as dead. Minerva Goldberg has used all her matchmaking wiles to make a conventional match for Clancy. Now it is time to use an unconventional one. Fashion editor, Carmen Pratka does Minerva a favor by going on a blind date with Clancy. Clancy refuses to acknowledge what the rest of the world knows. Carmen makes it her personal mission to not only convince Clancy that she is a lesbian and she, is the right woman for her.

*

Nocturnes
JD Glass

From acclaimed author, JD Glass, and featuring some of her most loved characters. Nocturnes is a collection of events and adventures, from the sensual dreamscape of the deepest love, to the brooding intensity of desire.

*

Paradox of Love
JM Dragon & Erin O'Reilly

Parker Davis's car limped its way into Portsmouth. It was just another city in a long line of places she'd traveled to but never settled down. The major repairs and debt caused by her vehicle, forced her to stay in the city and find employment with the local police department.

Olivia Santos lived for her work as a police officer, following a family tradition that she was proud of. The only thing that she would place above her police work was the love she had for her only living relative—her brother-an undercover cop.

When Parker and Olivia meet at a social function, there is an immediate attraction, which starts them on a road of passionate, unquenchable love. Their relationship binds them together in ways neither of them understand until a tragedy threatens the very fabric of their life together and their love. What happens will reflect on their future like an indelible stain forever.

E-Books, Print, Free e-books

Visit our website for more publications available online.

www.affinityebooks.com

Published by Affinity E-Book Press NZ Ltd

Canterbury, New Zealand

Registered Company 2517228

www.ingramcontent.com/pod-product-compliance
Lightning Source LLC
Chambersburg PA
CBHW071614030726
47598CB00001B/267